MADAME MORTE

HOSTED BY PIXIE P

BLACK
SHUCK
BOOKS

Black Shuck Books
www.BlackShuckBooks.co.uk

First published in Great Britain in 2018 by Black Shuck Books

Edited by Pixie P.

978-1-913038-30-4

The Tiger Lillies are a real band, whose songs are the inspiration for this story. It is to them, that Strings *is dedicated.*

There was a promise of something indulgent, exciting, mysterious even, in the envelope's soft, brushed surface and rich red hue. An exoticism heightened by the neat, cursive handwriting which spelled out Thomas Monroe's name and address on its front. There was no stamp, either adhesive or franked, which was odd. Neither had there been a request for payment of the postage amount by its deliverer; odder still in these days of no-money-no-service.

Monroe knew that its fascination would be short-lived. The envelope was sure to contain junk mail. Nevertheless, he opened it carefully. It was that sort of envelope, one you didn't want to tear apart with reckless abandon.

Inside there was a smooth, creamy-white card. Its legend was also handwritten.

Dear Mr Thomas Monroe

You are invited, gratis, to an evening of burlesque cabaret at the Theatre de la Nuit. This show plays for a short season only and features some of the most unique artistes in this world or any other.

The entertainment commences at the hour of nine of the clock. Please do not be tardy, as entry is not possible once the performance has begun. A table for one has been reserved in your name, and complimentary champagne will be served.

Yours sincerely
Madame Morte
Proprietor

There would, of course, be a catch. There always was. He examined the card, no clue, no corporate logo. Nothing. He dropped it onto the table beside his plate of half-eaten breakfast.

"Anything interesting?" Nina asked him.

Monroe looked up. His wife sat opposite him at the dining room table. She was dressed for work, smart white blouse, neat, black cardigan, hair bobbed and suspiciously blonde. Monroe was heading into early middle-age with resigned grace. Nina was fighting back.

Why Nina? What's the point? We're done. Time to step aside to let the new wave of beautiful young things take over...

"Junk mail," he said then glanced at his phone and checked the time. "I'd better be going."

There was still plenty of time, but he needed to get out.

More to the point, he needed to get away from Nina, who said "Me too," and got to her feet.

She kissed him on the lips, the contact warm and moist and loving. "Later," she whispered and touched his cheek. She headed for the door. Monroe knew he should be happy, euphoric even, that his wife of twenty-one years would breathe a perfume-scented promise into his ear before leaving for work and be waiting for him in their bedroom when he came home. Such a promise was, if the male conversation he heard at work was to be believed, as rare as a dodo egg.

So why wasn't he euphoric? Why did the thought make him tired, irritated even?

Nina was generous, warm, as attractive a woman as anyone could hope for. And yet...

He rode the tube, propped in position by the hordes of dead-eyed commuters. Then hurried along seething, rain-washed streets, past canyon walls of glass and steel, mind-numbed by the relentless hiss and roar of traffic. He entered his allotted monolith, rode the crowded lift to his floor and slumped at his desk in his 'pen'. He switched on his computer and prepared for the day's labour, prepared to make the world a better place by... what? What exactly was he contributing? What were any of them contributing in this sterile, bright-lit, slave galley? Projects to be run, reports written. And if they weren't? Would the world stop turning, society collapse, the universe cease to expand?

There was a picture of Nina on his desk. In the photograph, she wore a summer frock and big, broad-brimmed straw hat. She smiled her sparkling and delicious smile, the smile that he had fallen in love with.

So why didn't he feel that way now? What was she doing wrong? She held him and murmured to him and kissed him and touched him when he needed to be touched and yielded to him when he needed relief.

Nina yearned, he knew, for children. It was a quiet yearning, seldom spoken and never worn on her sleeve. Despite her career and wide circle of friends, she was lonely and saddened by their lack of offspring. Children disinterested Monroe. He saw them as a problem, a thorn-in-the-flesh that would ruin so much – their easy life, their freedom...

Their happiness?

Is that what they had? Happiness?

He would give in eventually. He knew he would, and for Nina, it would be the final piece in her jigsaw of contentment.

Monroe took off his coat, reached into the pocket for his phone and found the envelope. He had no recollection of putting it there. The last he remembered of it, he was going to file the thing under "Mail, Junk", in the recycle bin under the kitchen sink.

He frowned, drew out the card and lay it on the desk by his computer. Then went to make his first work coffee.

"I'm really sorry Nina, a new project... urgent. I have to stay late."

A sigh, followed by a reluctant "I understand." Nina chuckled over the phone and offered a second, comically dramatic sigh. "Here I am sprawled across the bed, all lipstick, stockings and high heels, and you've got to work... what's a poor girl to do?"

"Stay exactly where you are, don't you dare move an inch." Monroe hoped his fake lust was convincing.

She chuckled again. "Oh, you're such a brute."

Guilt sliced through his irritation. He didn't want to hurt her. She didn't deserve that.

Despite the address on the card, the Theatre de la Nuit was hard to locate, even for a Knowledge-possessed cabbie. When the car swung into the road specified, Monroe's heart sank. It was a dead street, a region of decay, of boarded-up windows and mindless graffiti, ill-served and shadow-strewn by the few of its street lamps that actually worked. He had been conned, made a fool of, or worse, led into a trap by a gang of muggers.

Then he saw the glow that tore open the derelict heart of the place and knew that it was real and that he had arrived.

The theatre was a palace of restlessly dancing light and shade, of intimacy and grandeur, a confusing palette of fractured impression. Its foyer and grand staircase thronged with the evening's audience, many of whom were imposing in expensive fur and evening-wear. Monroe felt shabby and stale in his work-worn office suit. Embarrassed, he headed for the auditorium and his table-for-one.

This turned out to be in a prime position, close, and central, to the stage. The table was small and decorated with red cloth, gently flickering candle and, as promised, complimentary glass of champagne. The corners and boundaries of the theatre were hidden in shadow, which created an impression of great size, of titanic chandeliers, of balconies, private boxes, fluted columns and gold leaf. The stage itself was concealed behind immense scarlet curtains. An orchestra tuned-up, unseen, in their pit. The audience talked and laughed and the atmosphere grew tight with anticipation.

The curtain twitched and a figure emerged, tall, elegant in white bow tie and tails. His cheekbones were high and razor sharp, his lips curved into what looked to be an everlasting sneer of disapproval. His manner was languid. He held a cigarette between slender fingers.

A cigarette? In a public place?

Oddly refreshing, an act of defiance Monroe approved of.

"Good evening," the man drawled, "and welcome to the Theatre de la Nuit's Dark Burlesque. For this enchanted evening, I am your interlocutor, your host and your friend."

There was applause, enthusiastic enough for Monroe to believe that most of the audience were regulars who understood the rules and etiquette of this place. Strictures, he sensed, that were complex and immutable.

"And so, to the first of this evening's entertainments." The Interlocutor smiled faintly and peered out at the audience, as if gauging their fitness to receive his theatrical bounty. "A musical ensemble of a most delightfully wicked kind. The Tiger Lillies."

A cheer. The curtain swept open to reveal a trio, three men, each daubed with the kind of clown make-up used only in the circus of a nightmare. There was a double bass, a drum kit and at the centre, an accordion player who set the group into life with a tango rhythm against which he sang, in a startling *bel canto* voice, a song of gin and sin, of prostitutes and pimps and thieves, all flavoured with a strange sense of tragedy and loss. Monroe was deliciously appalled as the songs reached into the darker parts of his soul and found union.

Next there was an acrobat; a woman who, it seemed, had little in the way of bone or joint. She was followed by a magician and his assistant who, chained and hooded was lowered head first into a glass tank of what her master had claimed to be sulphuric acid, a claim apparently proven as the woman's flesh reddened, then blistered then erupted and melted. There were cries from the auditorium, Monroe surged to his feet, horrified, feeling sick –

She was hoisted out.

Whole, unblemished.

Smiling her impeccable, white-enamel smile.

A crash of symbol, a roll of drum then The Interlocutor glided, once more, from the shadows.

"Ladies, gentlemen, and all between and beyond," he purred. "For your delectation and delight and for your adoration, the beautiful, the tragic, Lania!"

He moved aside, arm extended into the well of darkness revealed by the swiftly parting curtains. A darkness, pregnant with possibilities, and that seemed to hold the audience in a hush so taut Monroe feared some communal vessel would burst and haemorrhage in a flood of violent, hair-tearing emotion.

The darkness was sliced apart by a single red down-light.

Lania.

For a moment, Monroe couldn't understand what he saw. Lania stood alone, head bowed, arms crossed over her breasts in the manner of a formal corpse. She wore a dress that reminded him of gypsies and of flamenco, and it was as black as the hair that tumbled, lushly, about her face and shoulders. When her head snapped up and she spread her arms wide and high, crucifix-style, Monroe's bewilderment increased. The movement was... wrong. There was an odd jerkiness to it, something mechanical.

And her face.

It was beautiful, yet exaggerated, her dark, dark eyes, her rich, ruby lips, all too large—

here I am sprawled across the bed, all lipstick, stockings and high heels, and you've got to work... what's a poor girl to do?

—and frozen into an expression of sadness and loss that gave her an erotically-charged vulnerability. As she began her dance, and even before he glimpsed the silvery threads linking her to the impenetrable shadow above the glare of stage lighting, Monroe understood that Lania was a life-size marionette. A thing of wood, steel and paint.

The music to which she danced was provided by the Tiger Lillies, and began as a lament, pierced by an accompanying violin, and punctuated with the anguished respiration of an accordion.

Her dance grew in intensity as the music accelerated towards some far-off climax. Her dance was sinuous movement, feline, serpentine, it became furious, pirouettes so fast her body blurred into a grey tornado of outstretched arms and swirled hair, she stalked and leapt, tumbling impossibly as she threw herself—

herself? She could do nothing herself, surely she was the plaything of her puppeteer

—to the floor, where she crawled and writhed then arched her body and clawed at some imaginary lover.

What's a poor girl to do Tom?

And as each moment passed, Monroe felt himself fall deeper and deeper into the illusion until all mechanical artifice had faded and Lania became a thing of fragile, tormented flesh. The performance unsettled him, drew tears into his eyes and, more disturbing still, electric shocks of desire through his nerves.

It ended, as it began, Lania at the front of the stage, head thrown back, arms pinioned to some imaginary cross. She bowed, the action graceful.

Then, when she once more lifted her head, Monroe was sure that he was the focus of her frozen, paint-on-wood stare. The stare was filled with longing, sadness. The stare was a plea.

What's a poor girl to do? Tom? Tom, are you listening to me? Tom?

As the auditorium resounded to the deafening storm of cheers and applause and the synchronised surge of bodies coming to a standing ovation, Lania stepped gracefully back to allow the curtains to sweep shut.

And, in the last seconds, as the gap was about to close, Monroe saw her jerked roughly and carelessly backwards into the shadow and there was a moment, a ridiculous and mad moment, in which he was sure he saw pain and humiliation.

The dance ends and she stands, crucified on her invisible gibbet, at the front of the stage as the audience roar in delight. Monroe is there, hands sore from clapping, throat torn by cheering. This time, though, his euphoria turns to panic. The curtains are closing. He has to get to her, before that moment, before that final, terrible, jolt that wrenches her away from him and into the darkness.

He claws his way through the crowd, hemmed in, desperate, barely able to breathe. Fighting off hands that grasp at him and tear at his clothes, that uncurl, tentacle-like from the orchestra pit, he climbs onto the stage and hurls himself through the momentary sliver of black between the onrushing curtains.

She stands, face a mask of desolation. He cries out her name and lunges towards her. He feels her hands, wooden, unyielding, yet warm. He feels her fingers close about his.

Then he hears the heartbeat. A deep rhythm that pulses from the deeper darkness above them. It grows louder, thrums through his skull, through his flesh. The sound of it cracks bone, shreds nerves. Weakens his grip.

Until

Lania is wrenched away from him in a tortured clatter of wood and rustling taffeta.

He cries out her name –

"Huh…Whuh…Wha' did you say?" Nina mumbled sleepily.

Monroe, suddenly awake in the bed beside her, realised that he must have voiced his dream shout.

"Nothing," he sighed, feigning weariness. He reached for his wife and she settled into his arms, a warm, comfortable shape. There was no lipstick, stockings or heels. They were, no doubt, swapped for shapeless tee shirt and pyjama bottoms long before he came home.

After all, what was a poor girl to do when the clock struck midnight and her lover was nowhere to be found?

Monroe looked at his wife, who sat opposite to him at the dining room table, finishing her last cup of breakfast coffee. She was dressed for work, smart white blouse, cardigan, soft and green this morning, hair bobbed and suspiciously blonde.

Monroe glanced at his phone, checked the time. "I'd better be going."

There was still plenty of time, but he needed to get out.

He needed to get away from Nina, who said; "Me too," and got to her feet.

She kissed him on the lips, the contact warm and moist and loving. "Later?" she whispered. It was a question this time.

"I don't know...this project...It's only for a couple more days." His response startled him. There was no dark red envelope today, no second invitation to the Theatre de la Nuit.

He rode the tube, propped in position by the hordes of dead-eyed commuters. Then hurried along seething, rain-washed streets, past canyon walls of glass and steel, mind-numbed by the relentless hiss and roar of traffic. He entered his allotted monolith, rode the crowded lift to his floor and slumped at his desk in his 'pen'. He switched on his computer and prepared to work.

A meeting was called. In one of the goldfish bowl

conference rooms, the oh-so-young departmental manager fed them a generic spiel littered with the very latest in management phrasing. In return, the assembled underlings demonstrated their own cliché-awareness. Monroe became aware that he had been asked a question.

"I'm sorry?"

"The Grown-Up-Dot-Joined-Thinking Plan, have you finished it yet?"

"Uh, almost–"

A moment, redolent with carefully manicured, managerial annoyance.

"It should have been delivered to the review team two days ago Tom."

Mister Monroe to you, Sonny. Show some respect for your elders and betters you acne-ridden whelp.

"I know but–"

"Tom, Gup-Deejay-Peetee is a keystone project. There's no milestone-manoeuvrability here. We need that plan."

"I know—"

"I think you and I need some personalised face-to-face. There are obviously issues here."

Class was dismissed, Monroe asked to stay behind.

"What's going on Tom?" Voice and body-language carefully adjusted to the 'matey' setting, hand on the shoulder, skilfully composed expression of concern.

Nothing that's any of your bloody business, Monroe wanted to say.

"You know, lost focus I suppose. I'll have it done by the end of play," he said instead.

"On my desk by four-thirty."

"Yes, yes, of course."

This time, he brought flowers. He didn't know why and he didn't think too deeply about it, either.

Despite his lack of neck, the Theatre de la Nuit's doorman cut a remarkably majestic figure in dark suit and bow tie. He frowned and asked Monroe for his invitation.

"I must have left it at home."

"Sorry sir," said the doorman and sounded as if he meant it.

"But, I really must go in—"

"Not wivvout an invitation sir."

"I'll buy a ticket. How much? It doesn't matter."

"Sir, I regret that you can't purchase—"

A second doorman appeared, as large and brutish as his colleague. There was a whispered exchange. The first man frowned, shrugged and said with a smirk. "It appears that Madame Morte 'as taken a personal interest in you. She says that you can go in. IF you feel that it's the right thing for you to do."

It was. He needed this. He had extinguished the miserable embers of his dignity today, in an effort to keep his job. He deserved this one indulgence.

He was shown to the same table.

Tonight's cabaret was again introduced by the gaunt-faced Interlocutor, but it was a different show, and Monroe's heart sank. The Tiger Lillies opened proceedings as before, with witty ditties about madness and murder, but the acts that followed were not the acts from the previous night. There was a juggler who threw and caught so fast, it seemed as if the white balls he used were transformed into human skulls; there was a set of twins, one male, the other female, who tumbled and cavorted but, at times, appeared to merge one with the other and form a single, androgynous creature. There was a fire-eater who blew flame from his nose, ears and eyes.

Then, as Monroe's mood reached its nadir and he began to contemplate leaving, The Interlocutor appeared one last time. He drawled a single name.

Lania.

The dance was the same, but somehow more frenetic as it neared its climax. Monroe was, once again, transfixed, and so nervous he could barely breathe. A voice yammered at him from some tiny niche at the back of his skull, to remind him that Lania was mere artifice. But the blood roar of his fascination was too loud, too red, for him to hear.

Again, she accepted her adoration in that crucifixion-pose.

Again the big, unblinking eyes locked with Monroe's.

Again, in those seconds before the curtains collided, she was yanked backwards, with what looked like deliberate cruelty.

"A little unusual, I must say, but I can't see no reason why not. I'll 'ave to stay wiv yer, of course."

"Yes, I understand." Monroe's mouth was too dry for sensible speech. He was also startled by the ease with which his wish was granted by the doorman at the theatre's stage entrance.

"Righto then. Follow me."

The doorman led Monroe into the maze of passageways that fed the machineries of performance like veins routing blood to the brain. There were scene shifters and chorus girls, people with clipboards and headphones and others carrying coils of cable. The place was all rush and hurry. Monroe recognised some of the evening's artistes, out of make-up, and, no doubt, headed for whatever hostelries might still be open at this hour.

They arrived at a door decorated with a small, painted star. Under the star, there was a name, printed on a card. Monroe was surprised to see that the card's legend was 'Lania', and not the unfamiliar name of her, as yet unseen, puppeteer.

The doorman swivelled his muscular bulk to face Monroe. "The flowers... You do, uh, understand that Lania's a puppitt. She ain't 'ooman sir."

Monroe nodded, power of speech finally dissipated by his tension. This was something he *had* to do, an act of madness he had to purge from his system before he returned to the grim uncertainties of the real world.

"All right then, you can go in, but you mustn't touch. I'll wait 'ere."

He opened the door, without knocking. Monroe took a steadying breath and went in, prepared to gush some lame explanation to Lania's owner and operator. Hopefully the man, or woman, would laugh, accept the flowers on the marionette's behalf and the whole thing would become a huge, amiable joke.

The room was as he had imagined such places to be.

Small, with a dresser, mirror and chair. The mirror was edged with light bulbs, all of them on.

There was no puppeteer.

Only Lania.

Who was slumped in the chair, facing the mirror.

She was slack and devoid of life, a careless mess of dead limbs and tangled strings, obviously dumped there by her heedless owner.

Monroe placed the flowers awkwardly on the dressing table. The doll merely sat, immobile. No heartbeat or breath stirred her chest. She still wore the drees. Her hair was lustrous and looked real, her perfect head tipped to one side on a neck that could not support it.

Her face was blank, yet not blank.

Monroe could see the grain. The texture.

Touch her.

The thought was a blow, a shock.

Touch her.

No, she…it…was not his to touch.

He moved closer and stared at the reflection of her face in the mirror. Her eyes were bleak, unblinking wells of blue. Monroe saw desolation and loneliness in those eyes.

He touched her.

And felt the lustrous texture of her hair. He touched her face. Its flesh was rough wood. There was no flicker of movement, no pulse or blood-warmth.

His fingers moved slowly, gently, over her lips -

Suddenly appalled at what he was doing, Monroe fled the room. He ran, not knowing which way to go.

A huge hand closed over his arm and yanked him to a halt. He yelped in terror and shock.

"Sir, sir, are you all right?" asked the doorman, breathless from pursuit.

Nina was waiting for him in the sitting room. She looked a little haggard. She was still dressed in her work clothes, though her shoes had been replaced by slippers. She held the soft green cardigan about herself as if for comfort. Monroe was both irritated and relieved to see her.

"I couldn't sleep," she said. "I'm worried about you, Tom."

"Worried?" Monroe's voice was tremulous. He didn't want this conversation. He needed to hide, in the dark, in his own sleep.

"You look tired, pale. This project..."

"Almost finished," Monroe answered without thought.

"How much longer? I miss you."

Please don't. Because I seldom miss you these days, I prefer to be alone, away from you. I'm suffocated, bored, irritated...

"One more night."

One more night? Why did there have to be one more night? Surely it was over, this madness.

"One more night," she said, and it sounded like a warning, an ultimatum. Then she stood, crossed to him and kissed him, open-mouthed and hot with tongue.

In the moments before he came, upstairs, in the superheated bedroom dark, he felt her flesh turn hard and grainy, and her hair transform into a nest of razor-thin, steel strings.

"But I have to."

"No one 'as to," said the doorman.

"You let me in last night."

"Last night was last night, sir."

"I need to come in. I need to see the show. Please!"

"No, sorry sir."

Monroe was exhausted from dream-sodden sleep, and from a day that had been a lie from the moment he had dressed for work and kissed a radiant Nina goodbye. After work, he had killed time wandering the streets. Cold, lonely, aimless and increasingly afraid.

And now this.

"I'll pay—"

"Please go away sir." The doorman's tone was no longer polite.

Monroe pulled his coat about himself and set off into the dark. Rain stung his face. He shivered and, for a moment, wanted nothing more than to go home. But suddenly, he was outside the stage door, with little memory of getting there. The door was, inexplicably, unguarded. No security. No watchful eye and, as far as he could tell, no CCTV.

He promised himself one attempt. If he failed, he would retreat and try to forget about this. If not...

He had no plan for afterwards.

The door was bound to be locked.

It wasn't.

Scarcely believing his luck, Monroe slid inside. The passageway was deserted. He saw a drum of electrical flex, and knew what to do. He took off his coat, jacket and tie, and shoved them into one of the passageway's many, darkened alcoves. Then he rolled up his shirt sleeves, hoisted the drum of flex under his arm and set off into the maze.

It wasn't long before he encountered the first clutch of dancing girls, resplendent in feathers and glitter. Then a pair of technicians, a woman with a clipboard, who was talking rapidly into a radio. More artistes; an elderly man with a ventriloquist's dummy, a stocky woman in a leotard, carrying a dumbbell as if it was a paper bag, a tall, slender, lugubrious-looking man in an evening suit who had to be a magician. Monroe fought to keep a look of hostile, busy-ness on his face, and avoided eye-contact.

He moved deeper into the labyrinth, always selecting the busiest corridors, hoping it would lead him to the stage.

He heard music. Saw the magician again, being hurried up a set of stairs by the woman with the clipboard. Monroe followed. And found himself in the wings, stage right. He was out of breath, and unnerved by the fact that he had made it this far without challenge or failure.

The magician's act climaxed in a flurry of white doves that soared upwards and vanished. He took his bow. The curtains closed to muffle the last of the applause, and the Interlocutor's next announcement.

Monroe could already feel her presence. She was a dark shape in the shadows that transformed his heartbeat into a series of sledgehammer blows.

The curtains opened to a wall of blackness, all view of the audience blanked by the glare of stage-lights.

On came the red downlight.

Lania stood, proud and elegant. Monroe's breath caught, his mouth dried.

The music ached into life. And her dance began, building towards that last, mad-dervish pirouette. The strings jerked like the strands of a fly-trapped web.

The music reached its crescendo. And stopped dead, freezing Lania into her crucifixion. The red spot returned and as the audience broke into cheering and applause, Lania, bowed then backed slowly from the front of the stage.

A heartbeat.

Monroe's own, loud in his ears.

The curtains rushed in.

And Monroe rushed out, the cutters had taken from his tool box that morning, were in his hand. There were cries of protest. Ignoring them, he caught Lania as she was yanked back, held her tight and snipped at the wires. The heartbeat grew louder and louder, pressure waves hammered down from above and beat at his skull. He didn't look up.

Snip.

Snip.

Snip...

The last of the strings snaked free, and, carrying Lania in his arms, Monroe ran. He barged past performers and technicians, who all seemed too startled to stop him. But something followed. It boiled out of the darkened stage, along the endless passageways. Its heartbeats thrummed through the air in rhythmic shockwaves.

Monroe stumbled on, out of breath, chest on fire.

The exit.

Monroe lurched towards the door, crashed through and out into the street. Panting, he fell to his knees beneath a lone streetlamp. He clutched Lania to himself, trying to shield her from the icy rain. She clattered in his arms, a loose-jointed thing. Her strings hung about her and trailed in the puddle-ridden tarmac.

Monroe looked into her face. She stared back and there was softness in those sightless blue-eyes. He kissed the painted, pursed lips, and tasted their wooden sweetness and their heat.

He had to get her to a safe place. There was little time. The road shuddered under the beats of that monstrous heart. Monroe stood and a foot clattered onto the road, a hand, a leg. Lania was shattering in his grasp. He tried, frantically, to gather her parts together, to nurse them in his arms, but she was crumbling fast, as her ancient joints and mechanisms failed. He scrabbled at the fragments strewn across the wet tarmac, until his clothes were sodden and his fingers bloody.

Exhausted, sobbing, Monroe finally let her go.

He lurched to his feet, and as he stumbled away, glanced back at the theatre, but saw nothing, except the rain that scoured the ill-lit alleyway. Then he heard the heartbeat and felt pain in his own chest and it was as if it was being strangled by coils of steel string.

"The rich and powerful can have anything they can imagine," says Madame Morte. "But some things they *can't* imagine, and that is what we supply."

That's how I'd have liked to open my piece. If I could have got the proprietor of London's mysterious *Théâtre de la Nuit* to say it. If I could have got to meet her. Perhaps I did? As a master – or mistress – of disguise, she could have been anywhere in the place; where everyone is dressed up as something, where everyone is *acting*.

Though we journos are also actors. We live deception; and what we write, as everyone knows, is deception too. And we are seducers, as much as any theatrical diva, except that our goal isn't sex: it's conversation – conversation more revealing, open and unguarded than any mere bodily donations.

Obviously, we may sometimes need to have sex too.

"Madame does not like the publicity," Mantissa tells me. He has slipped out of his skirt and knickers and poses by the dressing-room mirror in his stockings. His bodice still exaggerates the size of his hips nicely, but his skin looks pale and his penis hangs folded and wrinkled like a slug. "The *Théâtre de la Nuit*," says Mantissa, "is for the direct experience." He looks at me firmly as he says this. "CCTV there is not," he says, "anywhere. No recording, no camera. The customers, they want to be free here. Doing anything. No camera."

On reflex, I touch my slim, specially-constructed eyebrow bar to check it is still in place. And filming.

"We have the business top peoples, royals top peoples, politics top peoples, religion top peoples. Dictator, Russia, film-star, billionaire top peoples." He pauses dramatically. "Darling, *everybody* top peoples comes."

That was not a theatrical 'darling'. It was the darling of lovers. I have told Mantissa that I am in love with him. He has told me the same. Tonight again, after the show, he will submit to the heavenly hurricane of my flawless body. It's not only that I'm fabulously, unfairly beautiful. It's not only that I'm original, stylish, fun and breathtakingly broad-minded. It's that, unlike most players in my superleague, I look and sound sympathetic and kind. If I acted to you, too, the heaven-sent lover who's incomprehensibly smitten by you and promises you everything, you too would give me and tell me anything. Including, of course, anything you shouldn't. At any cost to yourself. And that is what Mantissa is doing right now, in his changing-room behind the stage of the *Théâtre De La Nuit*.

Poor fellow.

"But not only the rich peoples comes," says Mantissa. "That would be very boring."

He rifles his handbag. He goes over to the cupboard and unwraps a syringe, and drips in some stiffener up to the fifteen millilitre mark.

He sits on the stool and spreads his legs. He holds himself steady with one hand while he angles the needle, ensuring it's empty before he withdraws it. He has to sit there a while before he gets up.

Nice angle. I raise my eyebrow, and my eyebrow bar rises with it.

Mantissa: his tall, slim physique, his dark wavy hair, his charming accent. Mantissa is very beautiful, although I have enough beauty in my life for him not to move me on that account. His rare morphology is extremely thrilling, likewise, but only sexually. "Madame does seek out, she sends invitation to most original, most beautiful…" Those few, Mantissa tells me, with a truly distinctive look or attitude or personality. "Like you, darling, for an instance."

"Goodness," I simper. "I'm honoured."

"Madame, you see, she is not interesting in money, except for it keeping the *Théâtre* to continue. She is artiste. We all is artistes. She is, you know, head artiste, or most brilliant from us. Most," he pauses a moment, "brilliant for disguise."

The super-rich peoples certainly do come. My own proprietor has, a number of times. He liked the *Théâtre de la Nuit.* He liked it very much. And when Max likes a thing, he also likes to own it.

Max Scrotstone in courtship mode – or in buyer mode, which is much the same thing – made the usual irresistible approaches. Madame Morte, he was informed, was unavailable. He made more – oh, indulge her whimsies of misbehaviour – but she *remained* unavailable. Which was a mistake. *No-one* is unavailable to Lord Max. Especially not some semi-amateur, kooky, small-scale club-proprietor. Unavailability is a major insult to his billions. His billions were offended. His billions will need to show the world the consequences of such an offence. So Madame Morte will soon be screaming her availability at his feet. He's a principled man. And the finest of those principles is to consign to Hell anyone who obstructs him.

That's why I work so hard for him.

I have fake net identities, fake names, fake friends, a fake flat, a fake life. Big organisations such as mine, backed by even bigger organisations, have fake everything. When the features editor talked me through the background, I had never heard of the *Théâtre.* The place didn't even have a website. I googled it and got *no* returns – which was kind of spooky. Still, I knew the job was important by the size of the permitted expenses.

I did my prelim. I used contacts in the tax system to look for employees. I used contacts in the banking system to seek out the cash-vulnerable. I used contacts in a telecoms provider to get psychological profiles built up from online usage. I zeroed in on a minor burlesque dancer, Mantissa, who'd worked there four years, long enough to know plenty, not long enough for loyalty. I chose to accidentally bump into him in Café Favela, Hoxton. I acted instantly smitten, but walked. Then, equally accidentally, we met again in the Gagosian, Britannia Street. I remembered him. We chatted. He offered coffee, his number. I looked hopelessly regretful, and walked. Then, amazingly accidentally, there we were in the Shoreditch Tesco Metro. "It seems like fate," I told him. By now, his imagination had done half the work. He was soon drowning, as I knew he would be. He told me he was a performer, though at first he was impressively secretive about where he worked.

Mantissa prods a few peps out of the bag onto his hand. The spike is taking effect and his penis now tentpoles impressively in his sequinned knickers. He dabs some rouge on his cheeks and carefully applies some eyeliner. He purses his lips and reddens them.

"We make showing our artistes as *unattainable*," says Mantissa. "As unattainable by *anyone*."

"You've not been unattainable," I say, fake-coy, flirtatious.

"This send our customers becoming wild. They cannot accept this. They is used to owning who they choose. They come back night then night then night. I have seen. They pays to be denied, to be powerless. It is the one thing they cannot have."

Nice line, I think. I could use that. Unless I get something better, later, from Madame herself.

I gave myself a lower-middle-class background like his. I was in finance, I told him, because then he would ask no more about my job. But I was getting out, I told him, because then he would know I had a soul. I mirrored his opinions, his interests, his preferences in bed. I played it fast and intense. I did the 'total openness' stuff. He told me about the background I had already researched: his troubled childhood, his love of drama, his indeterminacy, his realisation it could pay. He told me about Violet, the fellow performer whom he had dumped for me. And finally he started, after repeated prompting and a minor scene, to talk about his job.

"I cannot explain it," Mantissa said. "I cannot. You would having to come."

That suited me.

"The entrance cost is very expensive," Mantissa said. "It is impossibly, magically expensive." I liked that 'magically': Mantissa's imperfect English was often very creative. "But I can ask to Madame," he continued. "I will tell her you are so beautiful. So original. So wicked!" He smiled, and took a picture of me with his phone: my lithe, tall physique, my flawless face, the wheat-blonde of my perfect asymmetrical cut, my friendly, open look.

"Like audition," he said. "Of the invitation to be with us."

"Will I meet Madame?" I asked.

"Of course," he assured me, "if she is available."

It's not a prepossessing district: long-ago glamorous, then decayed, gangsterised, Bohemian, regenerated, reglamourised, and now back in the decayed stage; the streets around it ghosted with sweeps of weed-encroached precinct, the torn visages of dead boutique hotels, cracked panes of post-chichi brandchains; the mausoleum of an ex-after-hours resort.

The building gives away nothing on the outside. A brick monolith. A small steel door. Perhaps the effect is deliberately gauged, so that when you have handed your personalised invitation to the heavily-scarred young man behind his iron grille, and have followed the tunnel into complete darkness and suddenly blink to find yourself amongst the elaborate brocade, the burgundy plush, the tipped velvet, it all seems more intense, which it is.

The clothes you wish to dispense with are taken from you. Any you wish to assume are made available. You are offered, if you wish, the *Cocktail de la Nuit*, a cool light-blue colour.

I have an inkling of Max's takeover strategy. A breathy, heady, cooler-than-killing article that most venues would die for – and that I specialize in – will murder the *Théâtre*. Destroy its mystique, bring it into the public domain, and the top people – who come, as Mantissa avers, for the unaccountability, the freedom – will stop coming. Then, since it's these same people who presumably shield Madame Morte, it'll be possible and permissible to print scandal about her. *Inside The Top People's Sex Club: The Truth* is the usual genre of the follow-up. (The word 'sex', naturally, has to be in the headline. And 'truth': the word's like a damnation.)

Any scandal will do; preferably one involving Lord Scrotstone's enemies. The joint'll be investigated, closed, bought by Max for a song, and reopened under a *De La Nuit* branding: Tokyo, Paris, New York, L.A., surfing on the scandalous reputation we created, which the wannabes will love. Scrotstone International will broadcast how it's still secret and exclusive, so that every minor millionaire riffraff will slaver to mortgage their way in. It's one of my owner's favourite business models.

"So doesn't Madame worry," I'm enquiring innocently, "that she's vulnerable to predators?"

"Madame has defence," Mantissa replies with disdain, "of Art. It is powerful. And," he adds, as if unwillingly, "she has the protector."

Art, I think, yeah right.

"Protector?" I ask, more interested. "Who?"

But the door opens and it's Violet. She is, of course, stunning. She is wearing a demure, high-buttoned good-girl outfit far more sexy than any vamp effort, with a knee-length pleated skirt that will doubtless be repeatedly windswept and then fingered apart during the show.

She reaches out, and puts her hands on his nipples.

"Darling," she says to him, and unexpectedly I catch myself worrying that it isn't the theatrical 'darling'. "Can I have a word about the last scene?"

"Darling," Mantissa turns to me, and there's an

unusual authority in his voice. "You need to leave me now. The show will shortly begin."

I went out into the auditorium. In many kinds of club no-one will talk to you, but the *Théâtre* is, I suppose, *so* exclusive that its denizens don't feel the obligation to be exclusive themselves. I was as friendly and engaging as always, and was immediately chatted up by a couple of young men in see-through DJs and silk-scarlet hosiery.

"There is nowhere like it in the world," said the first. He was a dictator's son, from the Middle East.

"Madame Morte is a genius," said the second. His father owned 'all the trees in Russia', he said. "How does she do this?"

"Have you met her?" I asked. "Where is she?"

We scouted together among the super-rich and the super-original. I saw the Minister for Work and Duty, in a gown whose sequins were small diamonds, fondling the Shadow Chief Whip, who was living up to her title. They were both owned by Max. Yesterday the Minister had given a speech, reported approvingly in *The Smiler*, about the need for thrift and upright behaviour. There were the CEOs of Cockadoodle and DataGift, in morph masks. I saw Marque Stirling, the controversial multimillionaire artist, in his Nazi uniform. A society duchess in a crotchless leather all-in-one. The Twins, with their fused upper-torsos and multiple orifices. Another natural intersexer like my lover. And the entrancingly tall, the deliciously short, the sublimely thin, the fabulously disabled. Those with terrible deformations who redefine the idea of beauty in new ways, and have undergone horribly creative surgery for their uniqueness. Or those who have such uniquenesses as a gift of the genetic god. And of course the simply beautiful, provided that they are so achingly beautiful that it will physically pain you to look at them. Madame, I apprehended by now, sought them out, and kept them highly maintenanced by some inconceivable combination of pay, perks and pleasure.

While I was scrutinizing the assembly, I became aware that many of them had begun hushing, and that the band was playing more loudly, and a bank of surrounding mirrors were now reflecting the audience back on itself. Slowly amid this, the lighting dimmed to invisibility and, from far above, one of those horror-style bass-voices gravelled an announcement: *Welcome, Slave*, it boomed, *To Your Damnation*. Oddish, but evidently the title of tonight's spectacular.

At that moment the whole theatre shook as if in some tectonic tremor. It *was* a tremor – with an enormous crack, the *Théâtre*'s rococo ceiling split into pieces and started descending on us. The audience screamed. As it reached us the plaster became confetti, and melted away. The audience screamed again, with relief. Roofless above us, the night sparkled with stars. From one of them zapped a fireball that drowned the theatre with light, and as it receded, the stage was seeded with life.

I'd seen burlesque, *Gesamtkunstwerk, les folies*. I thought I knew what to expect. But everything from then on was a blur. I remember a sequence with spiders and huge snakes, a castle exploding onstage, multicoloured umbrellas, balloons like floating death's-heads – touch them and they shrieked and popped, to the amusement of the crowd. I was scanning for Mantissa in the motley chorus, but couldn't yet identify him. The stage sank into the floor and the auditorium rose slowly beneath us, as if we were the stage. And then another podium began rising behind us, though the mirrors made it difficult to judge. I hadn't expected such impressively – such 'magically' as Mantissa would say – hi-tech stagecraft, and it was making me dizzier than the earlier cocktail. At least, I thought, my eyebrow bar, my reliable, objective third eye, would be recording it all—

And just in time, I noticed the floor was folding away amidst us, spilling us backwards to avoid a sinkhole. The orchestra rallentandoed sombrely as from the pit, attended by very convincing forked lightning, ascended a cylindrical golden cage.

In the cage hung the diva, dressed in a long cloak rather like my own, swinging round and round from a noose, and thoroughly dead.

She was Mantissa.

My gasp was still half in my throat as the cage blew away outwards, the noose frayed and shredded, and a frantic psychedelically-lit dance number ensued, as my lover celebrated freedom or life or resurrection, giving me time to adjust to my astonishment. I'd understood that my informant was a mere subsidiary dancer. I hadn't even asked. But she was the star! I mean *he* was. So—

I am owned, I am branded, sang Mantissa, in fragile-but-defiant mode. *If I resist, I am tortured. If don't, I am damned. But you...*

Oh, that my-soul-is-completely-sold-but-you-could-still-save-me stuff. It's the kind of thing I was always a sucker for. Like many hard-boiled people, I indulge a sentimental musical taste; a reminder that I *could* still feel, if I chose. For my taste, the producer – whoever he or she was – couldn't have chosen better.

Stay away from me, Mantissa sang. *I warn you because I care for you.* It was an extraordinary voice. That wavering, those drawn-out sighs weren't put on; they had that pain-of-experience tang, of being what he represented, of every lover who understands they can never have the only thing they want. The dictator's son beside me moaned loudly, undergoing a desire, and a lack, he'd never felt in real life. *I am a creature of the Devil*, sang Mantissa. *I bear the mark.* I became achingly jealous of Violet as she scissored her legs around him, as she fought her hopeless good-Christian-girl battle, as the band ramped up another unresolved chord-change, and oh, that immense erection: I knew, I had seen, that it was chemical, but still believed in it. And I burned with a new jealousy – jealousy of the whole audience watching as he wrapped his now impossibly sinuous torso round a series of young-sweet-innocent clonettes.

I can tell, sang Mantissa, *that you too are lost. You*, sang Mantissa. *You. Me.* He was looking at me now. Directly. His gaze, of course, had that theatrical panoptic quality that makes everyone think they are the one singled out. But *I really was.*

You are as evil as I am, sang Mantissa. *We are made for each other.*

Explosions of fireworks, either in my head or outside it.

Crescendos. A *corps de ballet* of demons, pitchforks in hand. Money – actual money, twenty pound notes – falling from the ceiling, carpeting the floor. I picked one up – it looked real. My companion the dictator's son giggled at this desecration of the sacred quiddity. The forestry billionaire's son started stuffing them in his garter.

Let us hurt and destroy together, sang Mantissa and Violet in their union. It wasn't a tune I thought I knew, but found myself joining in. The whole audience were joining in. We all knew it; somewhere it had been sung at our cradles. These are the rewards, the audience choired, of our fantastic, our delicious evil.

Let us destroy, I was bellowing out, gazing up at Mantissa. Him, I realised. Him. Him! That unexceptional, semi-neurotic barbarian fem-hunk whom I had been pretending to love: it was him! I *did* love him! What had I done?

And the greatest reward is love, he sang at that moment; though the words were hazy. *Only the hateful can be loved. Only the damned can be saved.*

The money carpeting the floor, in the air, in people's pockets – caught fire. The stage, the audience, everywhere, became a sea of flame. The forestry billionaire's son was engulfed. The audience screamed.

Only the damned, everyone was singing, *can be saved.* Flames reached to our ears.

Him! *Only the truly wicked*, sang Mantissa, *can truly suffer love.*

It was hard to fight my way in to the dressing-room.

Mantissa was bedecked with flowers. A carnival of

audience, performers and staff were crowded around him while he acted modest and overwhelmed. As soon as he saw me, however, it was me he came towards. "Darling," he said. We held each other.

"But you're the star," I accused him. "You never told me!"

"Only tonight," said Mantissa. "But tonight I am the star."

Can you remember the first time you ever felt a new emotion? An emotion you had heard about, but had never experienced? An emotion, in my case, I'd heard sung about a million times, as we all have. I knew then. This wasn't lust, greed or desire for status. It was all-encompassing, emptying, exhilarating, a flowing-out like of something long-entrapped. It came from the stomach or perhaps the heart and spread through me like the artificial firestorm of the show.

"Come," said Mantissa. "Come with me and we are be private."

He took me firmly by the hand and, leaving the well-wishers quickly behind, led me away along a warren of backstage corridors, first strip-lit and breeze-blocked, then gas-lit and brick-walled, then torch-lit and stone-hewn, up and down long spiralling staircases of rock, iron and marble. We passed vaults and chambers, many, many of them, through whose openings I spied ballrooms, bedrooms, drawing-rooms, schoolrooms, offices, dungeons, attics and theatres of surgery and cruelty, like so many sybaritic stage-sets.

Finally we entered one: a cavernous, high-ceilinged *fin-de-siècle* Parisian boudoir with drapes hanging floor-to-ceiling, gilt-framed nudes, Louis-something chaises-longue in the deep burgundy velvet that seemed to be *Théâtre De La Nuit*'s signature décor, and an immense central bed. Faintly, I could hear music. I took off my cloak and began to kiss him.

Then I stopped. It felt wrong. Mantissa deserved—

"I need—" I began, and halted. "Mant, there's something about me I must tell you."

Mantissa was regarding me strangely. "Yes but first," he said, "take your clothes off."

Under his gaze I removed my miniskirt, my nippleless T-shirt, white suspenders, high heels, knickers.

Mant's fingers delicately etched my face.

"Now," he whispered, "Tell me."

No more lies; no more deception. I would be truthful. Terrifying, but I had to – for both of us.

"It's something awful."

My voice sounded louder, and echoey, as though a microphone were attached to it.

He nodded encouragingly.

"I'm not an investment banker," I sang out. "I'm a journalist. For *The Smiler*."

Mantissa's response was again gently to touch my face. Delicately – with the delicacy with which he did everything – he was gripping the barbell of my eyebrow-piece and unscrewing the ball. Then he took a pair of pincers in his other hand, and crushed the micro-camera in its jaws.

A coldness went through my stomach. I looked up, and saw that the full-length curtains had silently opened. Somewhere in the pit below, shadowed faces were gaping darkly at us. And almost before I could take this in, the other three walls sank away, each exhuming another silent congregation.

We were *on stage*. Our bedded island was surrounded by a theatre of stares that had been witnessing my secret confession. And I understood.

The show had not yet ended.

"We know what you are," Mantissa stage-whispered to a sudden dramatic chord, "and what you are doing here."

Boo! jeered the audience. *Boo!* I could see now, near the front, the MPs, the Twins, my earlier companions, even the scarred doorman, and beyond them the seething cohorts of the rich and influential, the artistic, the original and the achingly beautiful, all sending waves of hatred crashing over me. *Boo! Hiss!* A few began to stand from their seats, as if preparing to surge towards the podium and tear me apart.

The band hit an intro: urgent, desperate, lost. *I have been a fake,* I sang urgently, into the tumult. *I have been acting,* I sang to Mantissa and everyone. *I have pretended to love you. I have intended to destroy you.* A chord-change with a long-drawn bassoon note prompted me to add: *And for what?*

Madame, sang a chorus of slutty angels around me, *is protected by a greater power than Lord Max Scrotstone.*

But now I am yours, I sang in counterpoint, to everyone and to Mantissa. *I am yours in heart and soul.*

Ahh, said the audience, their mood modulating like the key, their transmuted waves of sympathy and forgiveness almost physical.

Now you are ours, sang the company, *in the great, the endless show of the hopelessly damned.*

And there in the audience, suddenly spot-lit, was Max. Laughing, among acquaintances who were also laughing. Amused to be mentioned, to be the focus of a jester's joke.

There is a greater one than Max, the chorus reprised. *Honest!*

More laughter from the audience. A shotburst of clapping, and another bold key-change. *Only the damned can sing without fear*, anthemed in one voice the whole company and audience. *Because for the damned*, they sang, *the worst has already happened. There is no hope. But you are ours. We are yours. We are damned but to love.*

Great powerchords of exultation fired from the brass section as a trio of dancers lifted me high above their heads, twirled me around and threw me through the air. I flew over the heads of the open-mouthed audience, over their raised arms and multi-coloured costumes, and their fingertips brushed my naked stomach and thighs. I flew. I flew into the darkness at the end of the auditorium or beyond it and it was like the *Théâtre*'s red velvet was an open mouth and ahead was its flesh-walled throat as dark as its entrance, and I saw something – something I can't speak of, coming towards me.

The sun was high. I could see a slab of blue sky between the shadowed verticals of buildings. I was outside, on an oil-stained patch of asphalt beside a cluster of plastic trashbins. There was the distant sound of traffic.

"Mantissa," I spoke out loud, as my memory returned

like the firebolt from the spectacle. The choruses of spiders and snakes, mirthful demons and unchaste angels, the undiscoverable Madame Morte, my uncloaking, the destruction of my micro-camera, my burlesqued recantation, my unattainable Mantissa, Max in the audience, the piece I was supposed to write, that I had still to produce.

I stood up, and ventured out of the alley onto the silent street. The theatre offered back its inscrutable facade. I looked into the cracked pane of the empty shop-window opposite, and my new identity looked back. I was wearing, somehow, a skin-coloured bodystocking, a theatrical nudity. My body was still lithe and tall. My hair was still in its perfect asymmetrical cut. It was my face they had chosen. Over my perfect skin had been carved – or branded, or etched – a mask-wide capital 'M'. Its central V ran from eyebrows to chin, its livid uprights down through my eyes like clowns' make-up, and on down my cheeks like permanent tears.

I was owned, and sold, and for a purpose.

I went towards the steel door, and watched it slowly open. I looked at the blue sky. I stepped forward. I heard the swing of the hinge, the knell of the metal, and the kiss of the eternal lock behind me.

There's nothing quite like Madame Morte's *Theatre de la Nuit* for washing the bitter taste of your own dismemberment out of your mouth. The tang of stale blood clings to the back of my throat and the agony of my most recent glorious demise haunts me in phantom pains and flashes of sense memory. At this point, it's just the thought of getting myself to the theatre that keeps me walking in a relatively straight line.

I've got a show to catch.

They've got Puck working the door tonight, doling out sharp-edged sass like it's going out of style. Catching my eye, he waves me forward with a wink from under the brim of his abbreviated top hat. I've never figured out for sure if 'Puck' is a nickname or if he's the real deal, but I've always liked him plenty just the same. If he wants to lie low, I'd be the last guy to drag him out into the spotlight.

"Well if it isn't Dion!" he greets me. "About damn time you crawled out from whatever rock you ended up under."

"Would've been back sooner, but I had to pull myself together again," I tell him with a dismissive shrug. "You know how it is."

I'm already drawing looks from the folks in the queue without actively trying. A few centuries back, I would have tried to work the whole 'body of a Greek god' angle for all it was worth. A couple millennia ago, I couldn't imagine anything else.

Tonight, it just makes me feel old and tired.

Well. Old*er*.

"Ember missed you too," Puck says, snapping me back to the present. The sound of her name makes something within me skitter with painful need. "We all did. The place is in serious need of a shot of Dion. Don't tell the boss, but things were on a *gentle decline* without you hanging around all the damn time."

I laugh and hardly even have to force it. "Nah, I bet it wasn't. But I'm here now. You can relax."

Puck grins and tips his hat, gracing me with a flash of elongated ears so quick I could've imagined it. He ushers me inside and I step through the doors into Madame Morte's.

Sound, sight and scent hit me with a one-two-three punch and I'm reeling.

The age-old smell of alcohol and sweat is tangled up with the cloudy musk of a smoke machine and a dozen varieties of cigarettes, cigars, even a hookah. The theatre is good enough to use a live band and the sweet little imperfections in the music send a thrill through me. I'm a messy kind of guy; I *want* to hear the subtle squeak of strings when the guitarist changes chords, and the way the drummer adds unexpected beats when the mood strikes him. I want to hear the music made ephemeral, how it's meant to be heard, only ever the same way once - not smashed onto a microchip for eternity like an insect under glass.

Or however that works. Never really got my head around the concept of digital recording.

The stage is awash in blue and green floodlights, midway through a number that involves a statuesque blonde lounging in giant clamshell. Back-up dancers in gauzy white silk cavort through a proliferation of bubbles. How's that for timing? I don't want to think about Aphrodite right now, don't want to *think* at all right now. The air rushes through the singer's lips and each sultry look over a bare shoulder is a spear pinning me in place. I could get drunk like this without touching a drop.

I move further in like I'm dancing and the theatre's my favourite partner, caught up in the sensory overload. As I brush past one of the round tables near the stage, a young woman bursts into effervescent giggles like a champagne bottle popped and spilling over. All around me, I know drinks are growing stronger in their chilled glasses. A well-dressed dark-haired man stumbles to his feet in my wake, laughing uncontrollably, convinced he can dance just as well as the beauties on stage. The music takes on a sharp edge, the drums coming through too loud, too fast. The dancing man starts whirling around and around, his elbow catching one of the drinks on the table and sending it flying to shatter on the floor in a spray of ancient wine...

Calm.

I take a breath, keeping my head down, and slip through the throng to my usual place as carefully as a glass statue.

Most people don't understand that parties are living things. They change and grow, rise and fall, hit their prime and eventually wither away. But the party within Madame Morte's is eternal. If booze and good music are a party's lifeblood, then I am its heart. And tonight I'm pumping straight adrenaline into its veins without even trying.

I lied to Puck on the way in: I haven't finished pulling myself together, not yet anyway. The missing part of me sings out from somewhere backstage, beating out its constant chorus: *I'm here, I'm here, come back for me.*

The lights fall dark, the music hits a final crescendo and the velvet curtain drops to a wave of applause.

The band strikes up a melodic accompaniment, generic, but still with that organic zest, a casual duet of guitar and light drums. I soak it in and settle back in my seat. There are some things worth waiting for, some moments that are sweet enough for even the poster child of instant gratification to savour.

From the corner of my eye, I watch two of the fishnet-and-feather clad servers engage in a ferocious silent battle over who's going to bring me my first drink. The process takes all of about ten seconds. It's the bubbly redhead who wins and sashays over with a wink and a glass. She sets it down in front of me; the red wine is so dark it looks violet in the half-light, kissing the brim of the glass. It's a minor miracle she got it to me without spilling a drop.

"With complements."

I force a smile and tilt my head to the shadows in thanks, but when the redhead moves to run a playful finger over my arm I shift away from her, a gentle but definitive rejection. I have to wonder if she's been briefed on me; she manages a graceful exit, though without the invitation I suspect she was hoping for. With a wave of my hand the drink flickers and goes clear, the wine returning from whence it came and leaving me with a chilled glass of water. It's about the gesture of offering your finest wine, not always the act of drinking the gift.

The chandeliers dim and the stage lights come up to dapple the curtain in soft purples and gold. A hush washes over the crowd, a swell of silence and anticipation; it's quieter than a graveyard in here, and it should be. The room is electric: drinks stop flowing, cigarettes burn down hanging from loose lips, the patrons poised, all anxious to watch the star performer of the *Theatre de la Nuit*.

The red curtain creaks as it lifts, adding a touch of nostalgia for those of us who remember when the curtain itself was young. The backlights soften and smoke rises, revealing a shadowy outline of the stage.

A staircase curves from the center to a bronze balcony lined with silhouettes: dark womanly physiques in seductive and over-accentuated poses, highlighting their voluptuous figures. But my eyes are drawn to the middle of the staircase, to the woman leaning on the glistening bronze rail. A little veil of smoke and shadow won't mask her from me. I'd know Ember if there were worlds between us.

Within seconds of the curtain rising I know there's not a single eye in the crowd that isn't on her. Even in this sea of sultry shadows she pulls every look. It's like being in the jungle and knowing a tiger is watching you; even if you don't see it, you're drawn to it.

My breath catches in my throat and I feel the hint of sweat beading on my forehead. I'm suddenly as nervous as a schoolboy in a brothel. No one dares breathe for fear of disrupting the moment that's fallen over the theatre like a silk blanket.

I want to sip my drink, but I don't move, because in this crowd with all eyes on her, I know the tigress has her hunting eyes on me. She's waiting. Letting the tension build to uncomfortable proportions, like a building orgasm, like a violin string stretched taut. I know I have the power to stop it, but I don't want to. I like it, this torture. It's been too long since she's looked at me and now I can't get enough.

Around me, the crowd shifts like a rising tide. Tongues on lips, nervous adjusting of collars, patting skin with napkins to wick sweat as the arousal builds. They gulp their drinks trying to cool the fires that grow in their bellies. They're caught in the betwixt of rumour and reality, anxious to know if all the legends about her are true.

I wait for it, until the tension grows to a critical mass then turn my attention fully back to the stage, lean back in my chair, and smile at her.

Ember, with all the aplomb of the starlet she is, doesn't move. A surge of anxiety washes over me. Maybe I misread the signs. Maybe she isn't looking at me.

Maybe I was gone too long this time and she's found a new lover.

Centuries of confidence melt away and the new death feels fresh again as pain twinges in my chest, a cruel reminder of the hollow spot beneath my ribs. Coldness roils through me and in the space of a breath I'm impossibly alone. I know I could have my table filled in a second with a flippant wave of my hand; the redhead would be back in half a heartbeat, but none of that matters. There's only one person I want at my table and now I'm convinced she isn't going to join me this time. My face falls.

A ghost of movement tugs at my soul and through the shadow, I see Ember's beautiful carmine lips curl into a smile.

Her first note carries, deep and haunting, growing until I can feel it reverberate through my bones. It swings into another, higher. And another. There's a pause between each beautiful sound and the crowd stirs in their silence, their souls aching for more. Her voice seeps through my skin, like a poison I know all too well and enjoy too much. It's like kerosene on the cinders that are only barely still burning inside me since my last time down, and I feel the flame ignite and start to grow.

The stage lights go up and the crowd roars; I pity the poor bastards who are seeing Ember's dangerous beauty for the first time. It's not something you come back from unchanged. Like a death.

She smiles and laughs, throwing her head back, taking the time to study the crowd section by section, meeting the eyes of every patron with uninterested scrutiny. Her predatory gaze falls on me for only a second before flickering by, but in that moment there's a flash – her persona vanishes like the sun behind a cloud and she lets me see her. The real her. Once her eyes move past me it's gone, her self-assured mask back in place and she takes a step down the staircase.

My confidence comes back, not as strong as it was, but a glimmer of what it used to be. I can feel the hold she has on me and I don't want out. I want her to squeeze harder, until it hurts, until I remember what living feels like.

Each calculated step draws the eyes of the crowd over her body and a part of me reels knowing they're looking at her. Lingering on her stocking legs and garter, envisioning their hands sliding up her skirt, salivating at the curve of her hips, fantasizing that they're the ones who get to slip their fingers through the lace of her synched violet corset, fixating on the sheen of the soft brown skin of her breasts. But I know they can never stop there, because her eyes pull you higher until you're met with the emerald irises of a queen. Those eyes... They chew your soul, spit you out, and make you beg for more.

The lights go dark and the crowd gasps. They get just enough time to fall in love and miss her when she's gone; try doing that for centuries. Ember laughs as the glow returns and rolls her eyes, tossing her brown hair over her shoulder. She purrs to the crowd as she slowly struts back to the staircase, making them give her everything and they do it without hesitation.

She's holding back when she gets to the first step, letting her girls on the balcony have some of the spotlight now that the crowd's primed. And then she starts to sing, drawing me in with a song I've never heard, something bittersweet about love and lust and wanting, and the band sweeps in to dance with her voice. Her audience won't be the same as they were before they watched her dance and heard her sing, but they'll be something new, something better, drunk on ideas and confidence.

My own fire is fuelled and I sip some water to cool off, but the inferno is out of control now. Each fleeting glance from her invigorates me like I've just been born again.

The crowd drinks her in like she's the finest wine of Athens. She helps them forget who they are and nudges them towards the person they want to be. She's the shining star of the *Theatre de la Nuit* because she takes you from the brink of whatever hell you find yourself in and brings you back to life. Hell, I'm sure that's why Madame Morte clings to her with a fearsome grip.

The audience watches Ember as they always have, but not one of them sees her the way I do. They see the consummate performer holding them effortlessly captive. But I know they miss the subtle tremor in her left hand and the sadness behind her eyes. It's impossible for them to see the desire for love and connection that claws at her from the inside, constantly fighting against her instincts that scream for the safety of isolation. We're the two most popular people in the room and yet without each other we'd be completely alone.

Ember slides off the stage, and immerses herself in the crowd like she's slipping into a warm bath. The urge to reach out and touch is written plain on a dozen faces, but nobody makes the first move – my girl's an untouchable thing. If they reach out to her, feel the warmth of her skin, the illusion could break. Nobody dares.

She slinks over to my lonely table, curling her fingers around my glass and lifting my water to her lips. I tilt my head to her in welcome, in reverence; she uses a single finger to lift my chin as she sets the water down, pressing her lips on my cheek for all to see, daring anyone to challenge this enigma. I suspect the shape of her lips is stamped on my skin as surely as she's claimed my glass with her mark. Some part of me wouldn't mind if it were branded there. The whole exchange takes less than ten seconds, but it's enough for whispers to spread through the crowd like wildfire as she makes her way back to the stage. I see Puck leaning in a shadow; he tips his hat again, eyes sparkling, and grins.

She dances until the witching hour and not a minute beyond; Ember's always been superstitious. It feels like a lifetime, yet not long enough. By the end, I can see the sweat dripping off of the performers, painting a rosy sheen on the paler skinned girls and the men who joined in for the last few numbers. Ember is glowing, radiant as sunlight. A muscled bear of a man comes up behind her and lifts her over his head at the knees. Jealousy churns in the pit of my stomach, but she ebbs the burn with a knowing smile in my direction.

She gives a final bow from his shoulder and the curtain sweeps down. The crowd is on their feet, cheering and screaming, reborn.

The band sets up a steady tune; as the name implies, the *Theatre de la Nuit* will be crackling with energy until the sun crawls back up the horizon. Groups slink off to darkened corners, making the most of their galvanized lives, anxious to test the new waters. Liquor flows and drugs make the rounds, both modern and ancient. I get to my feet and meet Puck in the corner.

"It's always something else when you're here," he muses. "Glad you're back, Dionysus."

He guides me to the back hallway, even though I know the way. We don't talk: neither of us have to be what's expected right now, so we walk in comfortable silence. He stops at the door and gives me another smile, knocking three times.

I can feel her before I can hear her. The door flings open and her arms wrap around my neck.

"Hello, handsome," she breathes.

I look for Puck to offer my thanks, but he's gone. Dissolved into shadow.

Abandoning propriety and façade, I wrap my arms around her and breathe her in. She's warm to the touch and it's the first sincere contact I've made since I came back. Maybe I'm getting as superstitious as her, but I always try to make sure she's the first woman I touch when I come back.

She lets me go and I wail on the inside. There's all of two feet between us and it manages to feel like a blizzard-swept tundra compared to her arms. I close the door behind us as she leads me into her dressing room.

The candles lighting the room gleam against her damp skin and the glitter on her costume, turning her into a resplendent thing. Most of the performers use those unnaturally bright bulbs to line their mirrors, but it's in Ember's sparkling firelight that I feel half-blinded.

"Well, what did you think?" She smiles, but turns from me and I know she's nervous. The woman who receives five-star reviews with nothing more than a modest smile still blushes when she asks me how well I thought she performed.

I move nearer to her, taking care not to close the space between us, leaning on the wooden vanity and leaving enough distance for her to meet me halfway. Makeup and paints are strewn all over the place in a comfortable chaos; I pick up the beautiful carmine she uses to stain her lips and slip it up my sleeve.

"One day you're going to burn this place down with those candles, darling." I'm drawing things out, trying to make her yearn for me the way I need her – the same way she played me on stage. But she's better at this game than I am; a part of me shatters when she looks back at me, the sadness behind her eyes more pronounced now, and I fear I've held out too long and hurt her.

"You can't get the contours right without the fire," she replies, but the life has gone out of her voice.

She moves next to me and I brush her cheek with my hand. I'm not good at this game at all. I give it up with a smile. "Best show I've seen from you here, but nothing compared to the first time I saw you. Dancing in the fire. That bonfire so high I thought it would singe the sky. Flames thrashing around you like whips, brushing your skin but never burning you. *That* was a sight to see."

Ember smiles, the life coming back into her eyes. "If I danced like that here, then this place really would burn down. You can only have a show like that on the savannah." She opens her mouth then closes it and moves over to a sealed trunk in the corner of the room.

"I wish you'd come before the show," she says as she unlocks the case. The black sheen over the wood glimmers like oil on water, but disappears as she speaks the words of her people: the poison barrier that protects the cargo inside soaks back into the stained wood. "The longer you're separated from it and the longer I wait for you to come get it, the more it weighs down on me."

"Like a burden?" I ask, disheartened.

"No," she clarifies, "like this'll be the time I disappoint you."

My hands reach for hers before the case is open, and I meet her emerald eyes. "Never in a hundred years."

"But maybe two hundred?" she asks, smiling.

"You haven't come close in more than that." I sigh, relaxing my shoulders. "Maybe it would be better if we don't do this anymore. It's not natural, Em." She holds my hands tight when I try to turn away, pulling me back to her.

"Coming back to life is as natural to you as breathing, Dion. Don't play coy with me. What's really on your mind?"

I close my eyes and rest my forehead on her shoulder. The heat of her skin is so soothing that staying that way for a couple of decades seems like paradise.

"I'm tired, Em. I'm just so tired." The quiet words slip out on a sigh. "Tired of coming back to a world that's twisting what I used to be. The Bacchanalia died out a long time back... This century's all poison and sharp edges, darling. My family's all gone down for that big sleep. I'm walking alone in the dark. The world's so different..."

"I'm with you, Dion, you're not walking alone. You've got a place here. It's more like the old days, isn't it? The way things used to be." Ember runs her fingers through my hair and I sink into her touch. "Isn't it enough to just be you? To just live and enjoy life?" She picks up my chin and tilts her head towards the trunk with a smile. "Now let's get you put back together, old man. Get some food in you, or send you back upstairs if that's your fancy. No sense wasting your trip."

She pulls away from me but this time it's my turn to hold her back. Somehow between being lost in who I am and getting lost in her is where I find myself. I smile and run my hand softly over her cheek, realizing that the reason I came back to Madame Morte's had nothing to do with the part of me stored in that trunk. "Why don't we get *you* something nice to eat," I suggest. "Some place small. Somewhere it can be just the two of us, for as long as we like."

Ember tilts her head and fixes me with a curious look. "But you need your heart, Dion" Shaking my head, I run her hands over my lips and give her fingers a gentle kiss. "When you're with me, so is my heart. Whether it's beating in my chest or in that damn box, it's still with you. That's all I need."

I hesitate but let her go and reach for her fox-skin jacket, taking the time to wrap it snugly around her.

I put my arm around her shoulders and she leans into me as we leave the dressing room. The sounds of the band and revelry bombard us as the door opens. From a distance, every party in history sounds the same. We could be anywhere and any-when.

"You sure you don't want to stick around here? Sounds like your kind of party."

"I didn't come here for a party, Em. I came here for you."

Ember cocks an eyebrow and gives me a sly fox-like smile, gesturing behind us to the trunk. "You sure you're okay leaving that thing behind?"

"As sure as I've ever been about anything." I smile and guide her down the hallway. We spill out together into the clean night air and I spare a glance up to the star-speckled sky, tracing out the constellations of all the foes and consorts that I've somehow managed to outlast. Not with fancy tricks or a stubborn soul, but simply by having something... some*one*... worth clawing my way back to each time.

It's a long overdue revelation I'm having here tonight: although my heart's not physically in my chest, it never had to be. It's not the literal organ that keeps me alive and coming back each time I die. It's the fact my heart's somewhere safe, held by loving hands. Time changes everything, not always for the worse, and it seems even after over a hundred cycles of life and death, you'll find there's more than one way to put yourself together again.

There came a tap-tap-tapping on the coffin lid.

"Ten minutes, Mr Eccles."

In the clammy darkness of the silk lined casket Tommy's eyes snapped wide. Breath rattled from him. He reached back and removed the pointed little finger bone that was jabbing at his side.

There came another tap on the lid.

"Can you hear me, Mr Eccles? You asked me to let you know when it was ten minutes before curtain call."

"I hear thee, lad," Tommy called back, cold hand pressing against the lid.

Rusted hinges creaked as the lid fell open. Tommy sat up, blinking against the overhead light. He heard the scurry of feet dashing across the floor, followed by the hurried slamming of the dressing room door. Tommy smirked. The lad had made a run for it as usual.

Tommy straightened his slightly wilting bow tie. After a momentary pause he clambered out of the coffin and sat down in front of the mirror. His face was grey and marbled with lightening forks of jagged blue vein. Eyes blank and rheumy. Lips ripening to an apple rot black.

The festering fingers on his fetid hands fumbled with his makeup kit. Slowly he applied foundation and rouge. Traced his eyebrows with black eyeliner. Touched up his eyelashes with mascara. Disguised the putrefaction of his lips with a dash of red greasepaint. Made it into a hideous smile.

Ghoulish, he thought, staring at the grinning reflection, *a ghoulish ghoul*. He reached for his pencil and pad, licked the lead with his green tinged tongue and jotted down the alliteration. Maybe there was a joke there – waiting to be extracted.

Tommy looked around the crumbling, plaster blown walls.

They were festooned in nostalgia. Brittle, age-yellowed posters from the music hall heyday of his career, reviews at the Hippodrome and the Tivoli and the National Standard. One wall dedicated to their provincial cousins, the New Theatre Oxford, the Liverpool Empire, the Coliseum in Airdrie and many more. His name was almost always somewhere near the top of the bill.

On the dresser sat a faded photograph within a discoloured frame. It depicted a stern faced woman, dressed in Edwardian clothing. Mrs Eccles. Tommy sighed. She'd had no appreciation whatsoever of his talent. It seemed to him her main purpose in life had been to berate and belittle him, making *him* out to be the bad one whenever he dared to stand up to her.

"You might be feckless, Tommy Eccles," she'd wail, if he argued back against her constant nagging. "But, I swear, there's a monster lurking inside you."

Tommy smiled.

She could never have guessed the full horror of what was waiting to be unleashed from within. The dreadful lust that seized him in the gut-soaked mud of the Somme. The horrendous and shameful appetites that had overwhelmed him as he wandered dazed and shell-shocked amongst the bloated corpses. The ravenous fiend he had eventually become.

But she sure as hell found out.

One rainy night after the end of the war, he'd turned up on the doorstep of the Blackpool B&B she'd had nagged him into buying for her. Oh the delight he'd experienced from the look of shock on her face when she'd seen him there. She'd been told that he was missing in action, presumed dead.

"I'm home for me dinner," he'd told her, pushing her forcefully into the hallway.

Once he'd gorged on her in an orgy of gleeful vengeance he'd kept her foot for luck. He still had it, wrinkled and wizened to the bone, amongst a gruesome jumble of trophies and souvenirs that had accumulated in his coffin.

He could scarcely believe it had almost been a hundred years since that night.

He'd stayed a few days at the B&B, devouring the guests one by one. For a while afterwards he'd skulked around dreary graveyards and prowled sanatoriums, frequently dining at the morticians slab. He was in no doubt that had the winds of fate not blown him toward the Theatre de la Nuit he would have perished long ago. After all, monsters have a propensity for being hunted down and destroyed.

But now he was under the protection of Madame Morte.

The deal was a good 'un. He glanced up at the calendar that hung next to his mirror. The day's date was circled in red. Tonight was *wages* night. Tommy chuckled and rubbed his hands together. Over the past week he'd worked up a fair old appetite. From a drawer he produced a fusty but neatly folded cotton napkin. He set this down on the dresser and then laid his knife and fork at the ready.

A tapping on the dressing room door interrupted his preparations.

"One minute call, Mr Eccles," said the boy.

"I hear thee, lad."

~

Tommy pressed his battered bowler down over his ears and tilted it at a slightly ridiculous angle. With a quick dust of the frayed lapels of his suit he headed out into the corridor. He could hear the wafting final refrain of a sultry torch song.

By the time he reached the wings Kathy Kelly, the Catford Contortionist, was bathed in yellow spotlight, naked as sin, limbs impossibly twisted into complicated erotic knots, a moulting feather boa serving as the thin line between artistic expression and gross indecency.

He heard a cheer go up as she unravelled herself and took her bow.

Sally B, the theatre's eternally youthful Mistress of Ceremonies, came on, resplendent in her tuxedo and cummerbund. Tommy prepared to make his entry, jumping a little when Kathy Kelly gave him a playful pinch on the bum as she bustled buxomly past.

From the stage Sally gave him a withering look. There was no love lost between the two of them. But he knew she was a consummate professional. She wouldn't let their shared animosity get in the way. The microphone whistled feedback as she grabbed it from the stand.

Tommy shook his head. *Never had microphones back in the day. A fella' had to learn to project his voice.*

"Now, folks, get ready to have your fancy well and truly tickled," announced Sally. "Here he is - the master of the bawdy rhyme, the Lancashire lad himself. Ladies and Gentlemen, the one and only, Tommy Eccles."

Cheers and clapping.

Sally turned to leave the stage, smiling smugly as if she was in on something he didn't know about. Tommy had no time to dwell on this. The band struck up the opening chords of his signature song. He entered stage right, one hand on his hat, pretended to trip on something, then looked out to the audience, feigning annoyance.

"Who put that there?"

He turned side stage and made as if he was calling to one of the stagehands.

"I said who put that there? I could have broken me ruddy neck."

A ripple of laughter emitted from those seated to the front of the stage. Not so much from those towards the back. Maybe the microphone wasn't such a bad idea after all. It whistled again as he removed it from the stand. Holding it up to his painted lips he launched into one of his legendary rhymes.

> *Mary found a severed limb*
> *All mangled up and bloody*
> *She'd have used it for something rather rude*
> *If the fingers weren't so muddy!*

Now the entire house erupted in vulgar laughter.

Tommy responded with his famous catch phrase.

"I always say that there's now't like a reet good laugh."

The audience cheered its familiarity.

One thing Tommy had learned over the years was that if the punters knew your material you could keep them in the palm of your hand - so long as you gave them what they wanted. He nodded to the bandleader down in the pit. The band struck up his signature tune again.

Tommy launched himself with gusto into the self-penned lyrics, inspired in no small measure by events leading up to the purchase of the infamous Blackpool B&B and probably every other bloody thing Mrs Eccles had nagged him into spending his hard earned cash on.

> *The price was right and so we bought it*
> *Then we went and found it cheaper somewhere else*
> *I said to her the day we bought it*
> *I bet we'll find it cheaper somewhere else*

But the price was right and so we bought it
Then we found it bloody cheaper somewhere else

The parts of the audience that knew the song joined in with the last line.

"Story of my ruddy life," quipped Tommy bitterly, when the band had quieted.

Old wounds never healed.

A heckler called out.

"Tell us a joke, buddy, because you sure can't sing!"

The accent sounded American.

It didn't do to let them get too uppity, even if they were on the VIP list. Tommy placed a festering hand on his hip and leaned forward, peering into the gloom. He clocked him, three rows back. He was dressed in a high-ranking military uniform. Next to him was an extremely tall and butch looking transvestite, face caked in badly applied make up, blond wig slightly off center.

"I know where you've been sticking your bloody bayonet," quipped Tommy. "I can see it in your eyes!"

Laughter surged like a wave from front row to back.

The transvestite pretended to blush. The yank officer turned and scowled at her. Tommy knew he had to pick up the pace. He had to keep the gags coming thick and fast. He cocked his head as if he was listening to something. "Here," he said. "Can you hear all that bangin' and thumpin'? Somebody's at it back stage wi' one of the dancers."

He turned around a called out. "Quieten down, pal. Make a bloke go deaf, so you could."

Pretending the audience couldn't hear him he stepped

closer to the front row and yelled into the microphone at the top of his voice, free hand cupped to the side his lips.

"I said they could make a bloke go bloody deaf!"

Again laughter rippled from front to back. Tommy angled himself slightly to the right. He decided to pick up a military theme in honour of the heckler. Make sure he didn't get the notion to call out any more jibes.

"She were only a corporal's daughter," he said. "But she went down a ruddy storm in the officers' mess."

Laughter and a few hoots and wolf whistles followed.

With barely a skip in beat Tommy threw them a limerick.

There was a young private from York
Who were peeing one night in the dark
He let out a yell
And cried what the hell?
When his mate stabbed his sausage wi' a fork.

A howl of hilarity went up when he recited the last line, mostly from the women.

"Here," said Tommy, "he didn't see that coming. I say – he didn't see that bloody coming."

More belly laughs echoed back at him from the crowd.

"You know what I always say?" asked Tommy.

"There's now't like a reet good laugh!" roared a section of the crowd.

"Knock, knock," went Tommy, keeping up the call and response theme.

"Who's there?" asked the crowd.

"Tsar," said Tommy.

"Tsar who?" asked the crowd.

Slurring his words Tommy weaved across the stage, affecting intoxication.

"Tsar's the last drink I'm 'avin'"

This time a cheer accompanied the laughter.

Tommy put his hand in his pocket and engaged the audience in a conversational tone, as if he were relaying a genuine anecdote.

"Who remembers the Great War?"

Silence.

"Well I knew a fella' came back from the trenches wi' two wooden legs. A zeppelin flew over his street and dropped a big ruddy incendiary bomb. Poor bugger burned to the ground before his 'ouse did."

More laughter.

"That weren't the 'alf of it," Tommy went on. "He's sitting there on his bum amongst the ashes of his legs and a copper comes along and arrests the poor sod for *arson*."

There followed a brief lull in the laughter before the double meaning sank in.

Tommy used the pause to scan the theatre for his wages.

He spotted near the back, seated with some of Madame Morte's regulars. Beneath the dull luminosity of the house lights the Madam's mark glowed greenly on the powdered flesh of her forehead. She was a redhead – voluptuous but not too top heavy. Tommy wondered what he'd done to please the Madam; usually his wages were either too stringy or laden with fat.

He smacked his lips and turned his attention back to the audience

"Are there any ladies in the house tonight?"

He saw some of the men turn to their escorts.

No one, it seemed, dared raise a hand.

Then the transvestite rose somewhat unsteadily to her feet, sloshing about a glass of champagne. "Here I am sweetie," she called, waving at Tommy and blowing him a dramatic kiss. Tommy grinned. Someone always took the bait. He affected a Scottish accent.

"I said ladies, no' *laddies*."

Another wave of laughter and another satisfying scowl from the yank.

Tommy cast a quick glance at his wages. She smiled demurely back at him. Madam Morte had clearly been to work on her. A promise of a place on the chorus line, followed by a bit of glam and mesmerising, was all it took. She was his now and ripe for the plucking. After the show she'd be at the door of Tommy's dressing room, eager to please.

Tommy felt his tummy rumble. Curdled saliva sloshed about in his mouth.

"Get on with it!" yelled the yank.

Tommy shot a cheeky wink at the transvestite.

"I think we're all wondering just what it is you'll be getting on with after the show." The laughter this time was a bit subdued. The audience were growing weary of the two-way point scoring. He couldn't afford to lose them now, so he launched into another of his naughty little rhymes.

Fe Fi Fo Fum
She's got a baby in her tum

Who put it in?
Little Johnny Green
Who hooked it out?
Old Mother Sprout

He placed his hand on his hip and brought the microphone up to his lips.

"Here," he said. "Can anyone tell me the difference between a seagull and a puppy?"

"They're both more entertaining than you," quipped the yank.

Tommy ignored him.

He held everyone for a few beats and gazed again at his wages. She gazed back and him and stroked a finger seductively down the furrow of her cleavage. Tommy began to drool. He imagined himself sinking his teeth into a plump pink breast and tearing away a bloody chunk of flesh.

A few impatient coughs from the front row snapped him back to attention.

"Got yer' flummoxed, have I?"

He paced the stage in one direction.

"The difference between a seagull and a puppy is..."

Another brief pause, then he turned and retraced his steps, head turned slightly to the audience.

"...One flits across the shore and the other shits across the floor."

Howls of satisfying laughter assailed him.

He reattached the microphone to the stand.

"That were fun," he said. "I always say there's now't like a reet good laugh."

They cheered the catch phrase.

Right on cue the band struck up reprise of his song. Before launching in to the words to bring his set to a close he gave his wages a little knowing nod. Her smile smouldered as she nodded back. His tummy rumbled a little more.

Then he was off, singing into the microphone and waving his other arm back and forth for the audience to join in.

> *The price was right and so we bought it*
> *Then we went and found it cheaper somewhere else*
> *I said to her the day we bought it*
> *I bet we'll find it cheaper somewhere else*
> *But the price was right and so we bought it*
> *Then we found it bloody cheaper somewhere else*

Tommy took a bow, headed to the side of the stage, stopped in his tracks as if he'd forgotten something, and hurried back to the microphone.

"Here," he said. "It's a long ruddy way to Tipperary."

As they cheered him off he cast a quick glance backwards just in time to see his wages rising lithely from her seat.

~

Tommy rushed past the scantily clad dancers waiting to replace him on stage. He heard Sally making her introductions. Once inside his dressing room he found himself pacing the floor.

He made his preparations. Unfolding his mildewed

napkin. Placing the fork to one side and the knife to the other. Quickly he covered his coffin with a crumpled blanket. It wouldn't do for her to get the frights too early. Wages had been known to make a run for it in the past.

He had a terrible habit of blowing them in one go, wolfing down the lot, so that he was left with only the marrow to suck from the bones till the next pay day. He fancied he would savour this one though, take her a little piece at time. Perhaps even take her in more ways than one. It had been a long time, but Tommy wasn't adverse to a little necrophilia every now and then.

When he saw the photo of his wife he angled it so that she would be facing the action. He liked to think that even the beyond the grave she could still be prudishly shocked by the wanton depravity he'd become capable of.

"Mr Eccles," called the boy's voice from out in the hall. "There's a lady admirer here to see you."

Tommy checked himself in the mirror. Removed his battered bowler. Patted down his stringy hair. Straighten his wilting bowtie. Gave himself a few squirts of cologne.

"Send her in," he called back.

The door swung inward. Tommy heard the slap of the boy's feet as he scampered down the hall. His wages stepped inside and pushed the door shut behind her. When she tossed her red hair back over her shoulders he was a bit taken aback to see that she seemed considerably older than she had under the dim lights of the theatre. Despite this she still looked a damn sight more appetising than the gristly nags and sows he was usually paid.

"You look delicious," he said, openly appraising her.

Any notion that he might have moved too fast and used the wrong term was quickly dispelled when she returned the compliment.

"So do you."

He stepped closer and brushed her powdered cheek with the back of his fingers. She turned her head slightly and took his index finger between her teeth. At first he thought she was being playfully seductive. But then she sank in her teeth and bit right through to the bone. Tommy let out a yelp and snatched his hand back. Tart blood fizzed from the wound.

Shocked he stumbled back against the covered coffin. She advanced on him. He saw how the flesh on her cheek, exposed when he'd rubbed away some of her make up, was as veined and marbled as his. She grinned and her teeth were black with rot. He looked into her eyes and saw that they swam with crimson bloodshot.

"Y-you're like me?" he stammered, hardly able to credit it was possible.

She licked his blood from her lips.

"I am here to inform you that your contract has been terminated. Effective immediately"

Tommy removed his bowtie and wrapped around his wounded finger. "She can't. It was signed in my blood."

She shook her head.

"You know as well as I do that Madam Morte can do as she damn well pleases. Your contract isn't worth the flayed flesh it was written on."

Tommy swallowed down the lump that rose in his throat.

"But why?"

She sighed as if the answer was obvious.

"Your material is dated," she said. "This is the 21st century, Tommy. Nobody tells jokes about the Great War. Nobody even calls it the Great War anymore"

"Seems like only yesterday to me," said Tommy.

"That's as maybe," she said, licking her lips. "But nobody finds your material funny. It's not snappy enough. It's not edgy enough."

Tommy felt himself stiffen.

"They were laughing the ruddy house down tonight, that's for sure."

She sighed and shook her head again.

"They were laughing at *you*, not your material. Some of them out of pity, a few of them out of misplaced loyalty. You're yesterday's man, Tommy Eccles. Your head is in the past. Your jokes are from the ark. You're crude and offensive and a teeny bit sexist. You're a throwback. There's a whole website dedicated to how shit you are."

Tommy grinned as a gag instantly formed in his head.

"Website?" he shot back. "The only internet I'm interested in is the one that goes in t'net at Accrington Stanley on a Saturday afternoon."

She huffed and rolled her bloodshot eyes.

"My point exactly."

"So you think you've got better material than me?" challenged Tommy.

A smug expression washed over her face. As it did more of the powder fell away, revealing the rampant rot beneath. Her stench rose over her perfume. It filled the dressing room, as thickly as his own stink filled his coffin when he lay down at night.

"Before the *appetites* seized me I had an excellent reputation on the stand up circuit," she boasted. "I was on the panel on Mock the Week once. Miss B was suitably impressed when I auditioned for her. She gave a glowing report to Madam Morte."

"I've been around a hell of a lot longer that Miss bloody B," growled Tommy. "Before she came here the highlight of her career was singing songs in her knickers at some cheap cabaret club in Berlin."

She looked him up and down and sneer formed on her cracked and fissured lips.

"I was thinking of wearing a scarlet basque," she replied. "With black stockings and suspenders. Finished off with some glossy red stilettos, heels as high as they go."

Tommy's hackles rose – Sally B sticking her damned oar in again. No wonder she'd looked so smug earlier on. "You can't do comedy dressed like that," he said.

"In case you hadn't noticed this is a burlesque club. Half the acts dress like that. On a good night half the audience dress like that – men included," she replied confidently.

"This isn't right," said Tommy. "I'm going t'see Madame Morte, right now."

He tried to barge past her, but she blocked his way.

"Madam Morte sees no-one. In any case her mind is made up. The price might have been right 'back int' day'. But now she's found it cheaper somewhere else."

Tommy balled his fists. The audacity, turning his own

words back on him. Why did women always do that? His wife, Sally bloody B, this one? His *wages* just stared him brazenly down.

"I'm a damn sight cheaper than you, Tommy," she said. One young man a month will do me. I like to hang them up by the ankles and leave them till they go a bit gamey."

Tommy's pent up anger flared. It was time to show this little upstart who was boss. His hand dipped swiftly into his jacket pocket and grabbed the knife that waited there.

He lunged at her.

But the blade of *his* knife was far shorter than the one on the knife which had suddenly appeared in *her* hand. He felt it penetrate his belly. She slashed up and then swiftly down, gutting him like a fish. As his knees buckled she swiped the blade across his neck, severing his windpipe.

Tommy dropped to the floor, gargling pink froth, oily blood widening from puddle to pool on the floor. He saw her step over his twitching body. He heard the chink of his cutlery as she picked it up. She sat down on the coffin, gloating over him, diligently tucking his napkin into her cleavage.

"Here's a joke for you, Tommy," she said, sharpening the blade of the dinner knife against the side of the fork. "It's as old as the hills, but I think, in the circumstances, you'll appreciate the irony of the sentiments."

"Did you hear the one about the young lady who invited the old codger to dinner?"

"'What's on the menu?' he asked."

"'You are,' she replied."

Tommy could only gargle blood as he struggled to prevent the rotting yards of his ancient intestines from slopping out over the floor. She stabbed the prongs of the fork forcefully into his cheek, sliced through the flesh with the sharpened blade of the knife, and raised the portion to her lips. Chewing noisily she swallowed and started to laugh. The laughter rose to a maniacal climax before she leaned in so close to his face that their ghoulish noses touched. "There's now't like a reet good laugh, Tommy," she taunted and stabbed the fork into his cheek once more.

Somewhere, Tommy fancied, Mrs Eccles was probably laughing too.

Richard scrutinised his reflection in the mirror, his eyes narrowing with displeasure as they focused on the murder of crow's feet that had started leaving their prints on his otherwise youthful face. He felt considerably happier about the distinguished grey around his temples that was beginning to spread and frame his face, not unbecoming, he thought, for a theatre director approaching his fifth decade. It gave him an air of authority, and Richard liked being in authority. Spritzing himself in cologne Richard patted his right hand inside jacket pocket. The ticket was there. It was going to be a good show; he had a director's instinct for these things, all the right ingredients; a personal invitation to Madame Morte's Theatre de La Nuit, champagne on the house and an opportunity to meet with the legend herself. Richard slipped his house keys into the pocket of his trousers and with one last glance at the sleek figure in the mirror, he pulled the door shut.

Theatre de la Nuit was, Richard mused, something of an enigma in the theatrical world; it was impossible to find anyone credible at any level in the industry who was prepared to say that they had been. Most feigned disinterest but it piqued everyone's curiosity, of that he was certain. There were rumours and stories aplenty. As a fledgling director Richard had been told that if Madame Morte invited you to her theatre, success in your career was guaranteed. He'd heard that Madame had connections in Hollywood and that being taken under her wing was a sign that big things were coming your way. Richard's step quickened with excitement as he approached the area that laid claim to the theatre. Although he knew where it should be, he had to admit that on every previous attempt to find the place, when curiosity had got the better of him, he'd found himself walking round in confused circles before finally giving up. He hoped that today was different; that he wouldn't screw up by doing something as stupid as getting lost, especially after all the care he took to ensure that his reputation was second to none.

Richard felt for the invitation again, it was still there in his pocket, should he pull it out just to check? That was preposterous, he told himself, it was there, and he knew it was, there was no need to check. Richard drew closer to the street which accommodated the theatre, his stomach rolling in nervous triumph as the theatre with its huge black door, polished brass handle and frosted glass panes appeared before him. How he had missed it before he didn't know. It was so damn obvious that Richard momentarily questioned his sanity; there it was nestling between an abandoned Victorian-looking chemist shop with its stylised snake and pole sign jutting out into the street and *Ye Olde Tavern*, and looking for all the world as though it had been there for centuries. The sign above the door that declared it to be 'Madame Morte's Theatre de La Nuit' was dazzlingly lit. He made a mental note to photograph it when he left.

Richard had worked in more theatres than he could remember, some modern and airy with state of the art stage lighting and sound equipment, some old and dusty with equipment that had, when it had been first dragged through the doors, already seen better days. Though they all had their own unique charm, this was Richard's favourite kind of theatre, the one where the show began as soon as the audience walked in through the door. The grand marble staircase with its runner of claret wool coiling its way up to the circle, the sparkling chandelier casting shadows on the hand painted ceiling and the framed signed pictures of stars of the stage and screen whispered class and success and money. Richard's smile of satisfaction was reflected back to him by the oversized mirror that graced the back wall of the lobby. He'd done it. He'd arrived, his future was looking bright.

The opulence of the auditorium did not disappoint, although Richard was surprised to see only five tables laid out with ice buckets and champagne flutes in front of the stage. He wondered who the other guests were going to be; if there were only five of them they must be big names. He set himself down at the table that held a card inscribed with 'Richard Burley' in a placeholder that had been fashioned to resemble a woman in burlesque costume. In another, lesser venue it would have looked cheap and tacky, but here amongst the deep red velvet curtains and the high backed cushioned leather chairs, they were nothing but classy. Richard sat down, poured himself a glass of champagne and waited for his fellow guests to arrive.

The second guest shuffled into the theatre looking confused, and as though he would have been more comfortable perusing dirty magazines in one of the seedy back street shops in Soho. Richard reminded himself not to judge a book by its cover as he smiled and raised a glass to his new companion, who in turn fidgeted uncomfortably with his glasses before finding a spot on the floor to study.

The next two arrived together, parting company down the middle of the walkway and heading in different directions to scrutinise the tables for their name cards. One was old, early seventies perhaps, walked with a stoop and looked like he'd had the life sucked out of him. The other was bald, mid-thirties, self-assured, cocky almost. He removed his jacket with a flourish before ostentatiously reading the label of the champagne bottle and pouring himself a glass. That made four of them. The table on the far right was still empty as the lights went down and the curtain rose.

Richard hadn't known what to expect, the invitation had given nothing away and with the stage in darkness it wasn't giving up any of its secrets either. If someone had put a gun to his head and asked him to predict what Madame might have laid on for this exclusive audience of four he might have suggested some kind of variety show, something that had echoes of an old music hall performance. Whatever it was, it was highly probable that Richard would have worked with a few of the performers; it was after all, a shallow pool of the genuinely talented, and he was sure that Madame would only work with the best of the best. Richard hoped, in the interests of his burgeoning relationship with Madame, that none of them would turn out to be one of the many young performers he himself had introduced to the business via the casting couch. Richard smiled to himself, perhaps she was the progressive type and might understand it as a perk of the job, lots of young, enthusiastic, inexperienced actors, keen to get on into the business and impress *the* Richard Burley. After tonight's liaison his value would no doubt go up and he'd likely get even more pussy. Richard sipped from his champagne glass, happily anticipating that the further up the ladder he got not only would the quantity increase, the quality would too. Soon it wouldn't be just wannabes, soon he'd have A-listers begging him to fuck them. Richard was aroused at the thought. If he worked it really carefully, in a year or so, when she was just legal, and Richard always stuck to the letter of the law where this was concerned, he could have that young girl who'd just been cast in the latest franchise. Catch her early, before the others spoil her, show her the ropes, literally. Although Richard laughed at his own joke, his arousal was becoming almost unbearable as the thought of his young virginal prey, her flesh bound and under his control, took up residence in his mind. Richard's fantasy was interrupted as the spotlight revealed a bestockinged beauty, complete with corset and Venetian mask, sitting astride a chair. Richard settled back to enjoy the spectacle.

He could see within seconds of her performance beginning why Madame had picked her. Her movements were hypnotic; Richard couldn't take his eyes off her, not even for a second, despite desperately wanting to see how the others were responding to this burlesque beauty. She flowed, Richard thought, watching her was like watching water flow over a pebble, perfect and smooth and without end or beginning.

Richard's eyes followed the roll of her delightfully pear-shaped hips as he imagined how he might bite them, his cock twitched as he thought of how the bruises, red and angry at first, would erupt on that alabaster flesh, turning a beautiful shade of dark red before later souring to black. Richard thought himself something of an artist, painting with pain on the bodies of beautiful women. He could tell instantly how they were going to be, how the quieter ones would, once the inevitability of the situation unfolded before them, submit. He liked bearing witness to their frightened eyes filling up with the tears that would soon be spilling onto their cheeks and rolling down to their chins. They never told, he made sure of that, once he'd taken a few photos and reminded them of the likely impact on their career if they were to find their way into the theatrical community. Or he'd remind them of the little movie they'd just made where naked and bound they'd begged him to fuck them after sucking his cock on their hands and knees. Though they would both know that she'd been forced into acting out his squalid little scenarios, the Internet would just see her as another cheap slut trying to fuck her way up the ladder.

The bolshie ones, the ones who needed a bit more taming, were Richard's favourites. No tears in their eyes just flashes of fire and venomous rage as they fought him every inch of the way. In the end they all submitted, Richard would always find their weakness, each and every one of them called him Master before they left that bedroom.

The dancer seemed to Richard to be performing just for him, her eyes locked onto his, her body swaying in time to the music. Richard was going to enjoy playing with this one. Perhaps he'd even get a private performance tonight. His mind treated him to a preview of the scene, her, still in her mask, bound to the purpose built hooks he'd installed on his wall, welts beginning to appear on her buttocks, the tears in her eyes having quenched the fire as she pleaded with him to stop. As his erection throbbed, Richard pulled himself up short; he was here to meet Madame, and that was his priority tonight. Suddenly aware of his surroundings Richard saw that the fifth table was now occupied. Its guest noticed his gaze and gently inclined her head towards him in acknowledgement before returning her attention once again to the stage. Though he could not make out any features in the darkness, there was a grace in her presence that meant it could only be Madame herself; this realisation was enough to return his cock to its flaccid state.

In his reverie, he'd failed to notice that the dancer had

removed yet another layer of her exotic covering and had discarded the feather boa that had graced her perfect neck. Richard was confused as to why she'd replaced it with rope and wondered what could be coming next. She took a few provocative steps towards him, his vision coming into sharper focus as the rope around her neck began to writhe. An involuntary shudder shook Richard's body, of all the things they could have done, they'd given her a snake. He'd never been able to understand the pairing of sexy dancers with snakes. Nothing was more likely to turn Richard off than seeing the object of his lust wrapped in these foul creatures.

The dancer wound her way towards Richard, swaying her hips, and holding the serpent above her head. His heart quickened, he didn't want that thing anywhere near him, the sweat that had beaded around his forehead and top lip was spreading across his whole body. Fight or flight he told himself, isn't that what they called it, when your body gears itself to run or to stand and fight? Richard could do neither, perhaps this was something Madame had set up for him, perhaps it was meant to test his mettle, but that would be ridiculous because Richard had made damn sure he never let anyone know of his phobia, weakness was exploited in this business. No, he was being ridiculous, this was part of the show, she'd dance her way over to him first, gyrate erotically in front of him for a few minutes, the snake would be dangerously close to him and then she'd move on to the other men. He'd than be able take a huge swig of his champagne and calm the fuck down in time for his meeting with Madame. All he had to do was keep it together for these next few minutes and he'd be a made man, a Hollywood director. His fear was nothing in comparison, he just had to stay in control of himself, remind himself that this was an irrational fear because it had to be safe, they wouldn't get a licence to have a dangerous animal in such close proximity to an audience. It was probably drugged anyway, judging by how slowly it was winding itself around her waist. If he could break eye contact with the girl now and look to his left, he'd be sure to see the other men looking at him, enjoying his discomfort but dreading their turn.

Except he couldn't break eye contact. There was no way he could turn his head away from the creature that was approaching him. Richard's skin crawled as he watched the snake coil itself around the dancer's outstretched right arm, disappear behind her back and reappear winding its way across her left arm. She moved still closer, holding his gaze as the serpent wound itself around her waist like a belt, its head directly in his line of sight. Someone must have turned the music up because he could feel the beat resounding in his chest. A loud rushing noise in Richard's ears reminded him, *it's just your heart rate accelerating, just the blood you can hear in your ears, he told himself, you're panicking. You need to calm down, take control.*

The snake slithered from the dancer's waist, down her right leg crossing over to her left at her slim ankles before travelling leisurely upward towards her belly. She bent forwards, her eyes now level with Richard's, her face close enough to kiss, as the creature encircled her one last time and dropped onto the floor by Richard's feet. He wanted to scream out, to run out of the theatre, down the stairs and back out in to the street where the only dangers to him would be familiar ones, the taxi-cabs, the late night junkies, the drunks looking for trouble. Richard could not move, as he felt the snake's body make contact with his ankles in this moment he understood what it meant to be truly petrified. Richard's only hope of getting out of this situation with any dignity would be if he could catch the eye of one the other men. If he could signal to them somehow that this was no joke and if they'd understand and in the spirit of comradeship intervene to get this damn creature away from him. Slowly, very, very slowly so as not to alert the snake to his intention Richard turned his head to the left side of the auditorium and as the fangs of the serpent created a deep red pattern on his body, the bodies of the other men began their slither towards him.

I see things other men don't see. Secret words repeated in mirrors, bits of legend fallen from the lips of slave girls.
From *Awakening Osiris. The Egyptian Book of the Dead.*
Translated by Normandi Ellis.

Phil's agent had suggested meeting here, a theatre in a part of London he'd never been to. It was inconvenient and he'd had to get a cab because, of course, he'd want a drink. But there was no question about not going, it was the first time his agent had contacted him in months.

"Aren't you Phil Jenks?" the cab driver said, clocking him as soon as he got in.

"Guilty as charged," said Phil.

"Blimey. I'll never forget that goal against Germany. Or the cup winner against Arsenal. You were bloody brilliant."

Phil tried not to read too much significance into the 'were'.

Then the driver started to talk about the case and how the girl would have been asking for it and that to then go claim she didn't want to afterwards... Well that was bloody typical.

Phil knew the driver was just trying to say what he thought Phil wanted to hear; Phil said nothing in reply.

When the cab finally parked up Phil gave the driver a fifty and told him to keep the change. He could barely afford it but the last thing he needed was it getting around that he was a skinflint.

The street was almost dark, the street lights not working, leaving only the illuminated frontage of the theatre. It was obviously the right place but Phil turned back to the cab just in time to see it pull away. He had wanted to get back in, to get away from here.

A silent rain came, tiny drops that he hardly noticed at first. He stood there looking at the theatre, at the foyer lit with ruby light, without a soul there. The rain collected in his hair, began to run down his face. At last he pulled the collar of his jacket up and walked towards the entrance.

Inside was a small lobby with a shuttered box office. The light stained everything with red hues: the floor scarlet, the shadows around the stairs crimson. From somewhere a figure approached.

"Mr Jenks?"

Phil thought it was a man but the face was soft, lips thin and delicate, eyes lined with kohl. The suit was a man's though, black and formal. The voice might be soft for a man or slightly deep for a woman.

"Yeah," Phil said.

"I'm Jay." Jay? J? It might have even been Jane. "I'll take you to your table."

And as Phil was led up the stairs he felt a fluttering of delicate fingers on his forearm, a caress that for some reason he didn't flinch from.

~

Emma, his agent, was waiting for him at a table near the stage. The room was dark, islands of rose light on other tables where people were chatting, drinking, waiting for the show to start. The size of the whole place was difficult to gauge.

J gave his arm a squeeze and Phil sat. J disappeared into the darkness.

"What the hell is this place, Emma?" Phil said.

The table was covered with a carmine cloth, and set with an ornate candelabra, its three stems adorned with the twisted figures of naked women, entwined like snakes. At the front of the room was a stage with a closed curtain, its golden folds picked out with red, the design of a great eye in silver.

"I thought it would make a change," Emma said, "and it's my treat."

He hadn't seen her for a while. She'd done something to her hair but he couldn't remember how it had been before. She was fit enough but had a rather hard face. He'd never fancied her, it made things easier.

"You said on the phone that you had a proposal for me. Where is it?"

He knew it wouldn't be in England, probably not in any of the European leagues either. If he tried to play football for any club where he was known it would all start up again: the press, the protests from fans groups and the local rent-a-mob feminists?

"Well," she said, "perhaps we should have a drink first."

Phil looked around. All the other tables were occupied with well-dressed people, some of the women were gorgeous, scrubbed up very nicely. He couldn't see a waiter but Emma hardly had to raise her hand before J appeared, glancing at Phil for a moment and giving him a thin, insinuating smile.

"Champagne, I think," Emma said.

"I'll have a scotch as well," said Phil.

And J vanished again.

"Well?" said Phil.

He wanted to know what it was she had for him.

From somewhere, very faint, there came a low note, some instrument he didn't recognise. Maybe Middle-Eastern. The note extended, didn't stop, and became a background drone that was pleasant, like someone stroking the inside of his head.

"It's a book," Emma said, "you tell your side of the story. What really happened..."

"A book?"

Is that what he really wanted to do? Sure he'd said it often enough. Sometimes he even regretted that the thing had never got to court. But a book?

"I wouldn't know where to start with a book," he said.

"Oh don't worry about that. We'd use a ghost writer... And who knows, this could be a way back, a way to clear yourself. Setting the record straight about what happened that night."

For just a moment he saw the girl on the bed of the hotel. Very drunk, rolling to the side as though she was going to be sick, her short skirt was riding up and he could see the backs of her thighs. She'd looked at him and...

The musical drone grew louder suddenly. Or else it had been gradual and he'd not noticed that some threshold had been crossed. He couldn't tell and for a moment he was confused, wondering where he was. He looked across the table at Emma who was looking back at him expectantly. The music erupted in a loud confusion of brass, drums and piano. People were standing, clapping as a spotlight picked out a band in the far corner. A soft hand ran along Phil's forearm and a whisky tumbler was put in his hand. J smiled down at him.

Phil gulped the whisky and then sipped the champagne as music filled the theatre. He thought it was jazz, a type of music he'd never really got. Wasn't music really just background for when you were drinking, dancing, shagging? But there was something about this music. He realised that he was waiting for an obvious note to follow the one he had just heard but instead the sax or trumpet would cascade through a whole series of other notes and then somehow return to the note he had originally expected. There was also the undercurrent of the drone, the strange instrument he didn't know. Definitely something eastern, yes. Then the beat of drums grew faster, the brass more raucous. Somehow the rhythm was kept just at the point it threatened to explode into chaos.

There was loud applause as the music continued and

Phil saw the curtain on the stage split. There was a woman there, her costume made of light, tiny spangles or perhaps mirrors that moved as she danced in time to the music, her arms and legs at angles. Long tassels spun around filled with light, and around her body tassels wrapped tightly to her.

When Phil looked at her he realised that she was the most beautiful woman he had ever seen. As she danced the rich darkness of her hair spun, its waves and curls like frothing black water.

He had to have her. He wanted so much more than to just devour her lithe body with his eyes as it moved enchained in the mirrored tassels. As he stared his eyes hurt a little but he couldn't look away. Then there was shift in the light so that different colours hit the mirrors and the dancer became a star of colours. She leapt, seemed to hang suspended in the air, her limbs spiralling as the music rose into a finale that threatened to become a discordant jumble. Then the curtain fell back and the dancer was gone.

The audience were standing, clapping and cheering as the music died.

"What?" said Phil.

"She was very good," said Emma.

A compare, suited and top-hatted appeared on the stage.

"Ladies and gentlemen, a big hand for Zalena, the Circassian Beauty..."

As a second round of cheers and applause rang out Phil found that he was standing, hands pressed down on the table.

"I need a piss," he mumbled.

Somehow he made his way through the tables, looking for a door that might lead backstage. He knew he had to see the woman, even if it was only for a moment to make sure she was real.

Somewhere near the back of the room he saw J.

"Hey," he said beckoning J over.

Low incidental music had started. Phil heard an act being announced but he didn't look back. He wasn't interested.

J was at his side.

"Look," said Phil, "I wonder if you can... the girl..."

J gave him that thin lipped smile, kohl eyes widening, whites turned the faintest red in the theatre lights.

"Zalena?" J said, "The Circassian woman? You want to see her?"

"Yes, yes. I've got money," said Phil, already rooting around in his pocket. It didn't matter if he blew it all, he had to do this.

"That is unnecessary," said J holding up a hand. "All you have to do is promise to do the right thing."

Phil looked at her for a moment. Was it this easy?

"Sure," he said.

And J took him by the hand and Phil followed dumbly through a side door disguised as a wall panel and into a narrow corridor lit by low electric lights. The walls were covered in faded velveteen wallpaper with swirling patterns of paisley, flowers and buds, odd abstracts making Phil think of the music from the theatre.

"You know," said J "about Circassian women?"

"Eh?" said Phil. He realised he was still holding J's hand. He let it go, flicked it away.

"Circassian women are reputed to be the most beautiful women in the world. Madame Morte always has at least one Circassian woman in her entourage. From the Middle Ages the women of the Caucuses were prized as concubines, taken by Genoan merchants as slaves to the seraglios of the Ottoman Sultan, the Persian Shah. The Mamluk rulers of Egypt, many of whom originated in the Caucuses, prized these women above all others..."

J talked on and although Phil was only half listening to the words themselves he imagined the scene in the harem, the naked slave girl newly delivered, chains around her ankles. She is being inspected in the most intimate ways... The rhythm of J's speech and the swirl of the wallpaper patterns merged with the melody of the distant music.

"The music..." Phil said.

J giggled. "There's no music here. We are too far away. We might as well be in the bowels of the Earth."

And she continued on, about the Circassian beauties of the Victorian side shows, of burlesque and P.T. Barnum, and Phil could picture them all, this succession of women, all ready for him, willing to do whatever he wanted.

J had stopped. They were in front of a door with an upper panel of frosted glass. They might have passed other doors but Phil didn't know.

J indicated the door with a raised palm.

"And I just go in?" Phil said.

"You just go in," said J and Phil felt his arm stroked again and J turned away and skipped childlike back up the corridor.

As Phil entered the room he thought that there must be some mistake. The light was harsh from a bare bulb and the room was a mess, a dresser spilling gaudy costumes from open drawers, other clothes on a chair next to it. The mirror on the dresser was dusty. Across the floor were blouses, shoes, underwear. There was a threadbare chaise longue and a curtain drawn across the length of the room. There was vague smell of old perfume.

"Who's there?" a voice called from behind the curtain.

This must be wrong. Some joke of J's, because the accent was broad cockney.

Phil took a step back towards the door.

"Sorry," he said, "I think I got the wrong room."

But then a head stuck out from the edge of the curtain. It was her, the hair unmistakable.

"Oh," she said, "I'll be with you in a minute."

"Sure," he said. He stood there not knowing what to do, fiddling in his pocket with his keys and loose change.

When she came out, opening the curtain just enough to make a gap, she was wearing a green kimono. She came over and took his hands.

"Come and sit down," she said, leading him to the chaise longue. She lifted clothes off the chair and threw them on the dresser. She pulled the chair up and sat in front of him.

"Did J bring you?" she asked.

"Yes," he said. He was a fool. He should go. Yet even in this fallen state of mundanity the woman was beautiful. He should still have her.

"You wanted Zalena," she said, "You wanted the Circassian beauty."

"Yes."

She played with a lock of her hair beside her ear and Phil knew he could easily forget the accent, the pretence of it all.

"Are you sure, dearie?" she said.

"It's all an act?" he said. But did it really matter?

"Well this is a theatre," she said.

With her thumb she idly opened a gap in the top of her kimono and Phil gazed at the flesh at the top of her clavicle. He edged forward imagining his hand there, how it would feel.

"Did you like the dancing?"

"Yes, I did, I..."

"What," she said, stretching out her leg and letting the kimono fall away from it, "did it make me desirable?"

"Yes, I saw you, I wanted you."

"Oh gawd," she said laughing, "I think you want the Circassian woman."

"But you..."

"No," she said. And she stood and dropped the kimono to the floor, letting it crumple among the other clothes there. Naked, she strode across the room to the curtain and disappeared inside. Phil was on his feet.

"Wait there," she called, "it's nearly time."

"Yes," he said.

He took a step closer to the curtain.

"Do you like women?" she asked from beyond the curtain.

It took a moment for him to register what she was saying and before he could think of a reply she added: "I don't think you do like women."

"Are you saying I'm gay?" he said. And he knew again that this was some sort of trick.

"Oh no," she said, "I'm not saying that at all."

She drew back the curtain and in the small dressing space she dazzled him.

The costume of tassels and mirrors wrapped around her, across her breasts and stomach, around her thighs. She spun and the looser tassels flared out with their reflected light flashing.

"Look," she said and her voice was strange now, an accent of far away. "Look and see what is there for you. Will you be in the harem of Topkapi Palace? The slave market in Cairo?"

Phil was kneeling on the floor before her. Each tiny mirror held a different scene and as his eyes were caught by one after another he was in different places and times. Then one of the images took him.

Somewhere a rhythm was playing, not the droning jazz of before but something more ordinary, something he thought he recognised.

It was from downstairs. The disco at the hotel the night that football team had arrived. Up here, in the hotel room, you could still hear the music but what she couldn't work out was how she'd got up here. She'd been dancing, drinking too much. And Phil Jenks had been talking to her, chatting her up. Of course she knew who he was. He was jubilant, it was an away victory and he'd scored the last minute winner. Very flash, full of himself.

It was good to lie down for a bit. She moved over to the edge of the bed and tried to lean over in case she vomited. As she did she caught movement and turned her head. He stood at the edge of the bed looking down at her. His hand was on his belt. He was saying something and she tried to tell him she wanted to go home but he just laughed. There was no humour in that laugh. Then he moved onto the bed.

Phil was kneeling on the floor next to the open curtain. For a moment he wondered where the Circassian woman was, then he rushed over to the little basin in the dressing area and retched. Nothing came out and yet he felt so sick, dirty, as though filth and slime had been smeared on the inner linings of his body. He heard himself sob.

He got to the chaise longue and lay down, his body aching. The knowledge of violation pressed down on him. He thought he might not be able to move. On the ceiling there were patterns in the flaking paint. He tried to focus on the patterns, not wanting to think. There was something in his hand; it had been there all the time, gripped hard, painful. He brought it up to his eyes and saw a tiny lozenge of mirror. Inside this, he knew, was that night. The night at the hotel when he had done what he had always told himself he hadn't. What he had always known he had.

At last he checked his phone for the time just as J came into the room.

"I think you are finished," said J, reaching down and helping him to his feet.

And Phil followed (slowly/in a confused state/questioning his sobriety?)back to the theatre where on the stage a woman was telling some sort of story, some sort of joke.

"You get lost?" Emma said as he slumped opposite her. He said nothing. There was a fresh glass of champagne and he swallowed it in one gulp. In his other hand he held the tiny mirror in his fingers.

There were cheers as the act came to an end but all Phil knew was the pressure of the mirror edges on his fingers. Inside was the hotel room, the girl lying there, him approaching her.

"Well," said Emma, "What do you think?"

"Huh?"

"About the book idea."

He held up the mirror to look at it, to see how the night at the hotel ended. Although he had always known. Always.

"What have you done?" Emma said.

"It's a mirror."

"What are you talking about? You've cut yourself."

He looked at his hand. There was blood all over his fingers where he'd been pierced. There was no little mirror. It was now somewhere inside.

"The book," he said at last, "yes. I want to do it. I want to say what happened. I want to do the right thing."

The musty velvet curtains parted revealing the spotlight blinding my eyes and the heavy breathing of the audience ahead – they knew what was coming. No matter how many times I performed, that spotlight always made me want to shield my eyes from it, but then I'd get to see the clientele and that was worse. At the start, nerves always played me like a fiddle, even after all these years. Then the music began, and brushing my nervousness away, I became the lustrous Valentine Divine...

Flicking the giant feathered fans away to reveal my curves and corset. Rising like a Venus from the chair and swishing the fans like a peacock tail behind, presenting my wriggling rump like a juicy steak on a plate...

I was good and I knew it. I could captivate an audience and make them hold their breath in unison until the lights went down; signalling when to applaud. I was top billing, so I knew they had really come to see me.

Laying back right across the chair with my right leg raised with a dancers pointed toe, tracing delicately but deliberately, downwards from knee to thigh...

The other girls were good, but I shone like a diamond, performing as if a magic gripped my soul and wouldn't let me stop. Despite the initial nerves rolling in my stomach, I only came alive when I danced; it was like I didn't exist until that first twirl or flick of the wrist. I danced for me, I danced for the audience and I danced for her, especially for HER. SHE was why I was here, and I wanted very much to please her. I owed her a debt. I owed her my life.

Gracefully getting up from the chair, turning it with a spin before straddling it with legs parted, showing a hint of red satin between my thighs, starting again to stroke my legs, upwards towards that silky triangle.

She'd found me when I had no one or nothing. She'd rescued me and given me hope, a job and home. I owed her everything and I knew I would give her everything, like so many of the other girls here. It was always girls she saved, I never really knew why. Maybe she'd lost a daughter. I often speculated about her; although she was our saviour, no one really knew anything about her.

Smoothly rolling the left stocking down and off, swishing it around and throwing it into the crowd, watching it fall gently into the lap of a businessman.

It was usually businessmen, politicians and bankers came here, only they could afford the prices, only they sought the prestige of the invitation to the club. You could tell one type from another by the suits they wore and the cologne they bathed in.

Unclipping the suspender on the left stocking in readiness to roll it down to share the others' fate...

Something had been troubling me though, something deep in the pit of my stomach, where the deepest fears are kept in check. What happened to the girls once they'd passed their sell by date – what happened then? I'd been too eager to learn the ropes to notice my predecessors leave. What had become of them?

Sashaying towards the audience, pulling the gloves off with my teeth, slowly, surely, one finger at a time...then draping it down seductively, across one breast, then the other and downwards between my legs.

Did she look after them once they'd gone or were they left on the scrapheap, just as she had found them? I was getting older and I needed to understand my fate. Although I was the best in my field, I was starting to feel the strain of performing night after night.

The other glove removed as sexily as the last. Pouring some wine into it, and then tipping it towards my mouth, some reaching its target and some escaping down my delicious cleavage. Every move measured, every move sensual to captivate and ensnare the audience.

It was taking more and more paint to cover these crow's feet. How long before she noticed?

Trailing a long finger across my red lips, blowing a kiss to the suit in the front row.

What was I going to do? I knew I couldn't hold this position of power forever. Maybe one of the punters would be nice. Nice? Who was I kidding, they just wanted a night with Valentine Divine, not the real me! Anyway, rule number one; don't date the clientele. So far I had been aloof to the plentiful declarations of love, flowers and jewellery. As often as I could, I'd send them back, but the anonymous gifts I would share amongst the other girls.

Turning my back towards the audience, rolling my shoulders with the rhythm of the song, slowly, deliberately starting to unhook the corset, whipping it up high in my right hand and deliberately dropping it down to the floor with a flick of the wrist. Slowly beginning to turn towards the audience...

What was that last one's name? Was I old enough now for my memory to be cranky too?

Arms crossed over my chest, hiding my heaving bosom. I let one arm rise gently and fall again, whilst my other arm still hides my modesty. I then swap arms, still being discreet, teasing the audience just that little bit longer. All they can see of me is my tiny silky red panties, dangling suspender belt and stiletto shoes.

Candie Box! That was her name, and boy had she been good. It was all coming back to me, like a fog had lifted from within my brain. I remember when I was 'the new girl' and watching her intently: she had been amazing, probably even better than I was now. She had been aloof, so I studied her style from a distance. I suddenly wondered, who out of the others girls here, now was doing the same with me?

Swinging both arms wide, revealing daring red love heart nipple tassels, I circle my hips and begin to tantalisingly twirl them around in unison, first one way and then the other, and finally, knowing that most burlesque girls can only swing them one way, I do the double swing, one tassel going right and the other moving left at the same time.

I suddenly remembered the last time I'd seen her, Candie. She'd just finished her set and found an envelope on her dressing table. Whatever was inside had made her cry. I remember big heartfelt sobs coming from her makeup stained face. The envelope had had the club's insignia on it. What a strange thing to forget. It was like something had stopped me from remembering these things, so I would be a good girl and do my job. Had I been a fool?

I turn my back to the audience once more, unclipping the suspender belt then seductively rolling down my red panties, again revealing my bottom to the ogling crowd. They are swiftly discarded into the audience and I carefully pick up the giant feathered fans, once again hiding my body. I love the feel of the feathers against my naked skin, it tickles and it tantalises. I don't mind the audience seeing my pleasure in this. I quickly switch the front feather to the back and the back to the front, daring the audience to see my bare flesh in between.

The lights went down and the applause was explosive. I always enjoyed performing, but I was tired and my feet were sore. I headed back to my dressing room. In the dim glow of the dressing table mirror's light bulbs I saw an envelope. On it was my name, and the club's insignia...

Mum cried all the way to her sister's.

Dad's fault. Again. I'd caught the tail end of their argument. The point when it became almost silent, other than the grunt of exertion and the sound of striking fists. The ups-and-downs of their relationship recorded in bruises upon our bodies.

I didn't want to go, but she did, and at twelve, I had no say.

I couldn't tell Mum that she'd chosen badly, and so too had her sister. For all I knew that was the way it was with everybody. Between them, they had a lot in common. Both married to violent men, only her sister had endured it longer and had raised two equally violent sons.

They didn't hit as hard as Dad, not yet, but it wouldn't be long.

Dumped on the doorstep, and pointed in the direction of

Old Kentish Town, I was told that my older delinquent cousins, Sebastian and Colin, were playing in the park.

That sounded a good place to avoid.

I waited on the threshold, wanting to leave my overnight bag in the house. As Mum was ushered inside beneath broken wings, the door closed on my face.

Taking my bag with me, I headed in the opposite direction.

~

I was looking through a newsagent's window when they found me. I realised as soon as I noticed that there were two extra reflections next to my own.

Sebastian was holding a neon Nerf gun, wearing a red boxing helmet. I saw them, but pretended I hadn't. I also had some boxing gear at home, but had only ever worn it to A&E. Dad used it to explain my injuries. So far, no one had noticed that the bloodied knuckles were on the wrong hands.

If I stared long enough into the glass, I thought, they would go away.

A strong hand clamped on the back of my neck and my head accelerated towards the unyielding surface. It ricocheted off with a bang and I saw stars.

"Hey Steven, you dip-shit."

I walked away, head throbbing, but I didn't want to give them the pleasure of knowing how much it hurt. I didn't even look at them. They were vampires. I'd learnt long ago that if I gave them nothing to feed on, their interest in me would wither and die. Gas Lighters, a term I'd picked up from one of Mum's self-help books.

I swallowed, and rubbed my head when I thought that I had enough distance in front of them.

I strode quickly, moving through side streets, keeping a mental bearing of how to get back to my Aunt's. But with each turn the surroundings looked less and less familiar. The last thing I wanted was to stop and ask directions. They kept pace, bouncing a tennis ball behind me. Sometimes it caught my heel, causing them both to shriek with laughter.

~

An hour, maybe longer, the torment continued. They'd started to throw the ball against my back, adding to the bruises that I already had there.

That's when I walked into a dead end.

Red brick walls of industrial units, decayed and derelict, blocked three sides. I stood at the dead end, facing forwards, unsure what to do. The tennis ball thwacked against the wall, returning to my tormentors, only to be hurled again, closer and closer.

I turned around.

The ball struck me and flew up and off at an angle, clattering against corrugated roof tiles.

Sebastian shook his head, "You have got to fetch that now."

"No." I replied.

"You were the last person to touch it." I hated him, hated him more than Dad. He said it as though we'd been in the middle of a game and it was an inconvenience to both of us. What did I care that it was lost?

The muscles twitched in Sebastian's jaw. He had the same tell as Dad, and my uncle.

This could give them the excuse they were waiting for. Unless I fetched their stupid ball, it was only going to make things worse.

I looked at the wall, and for once, they looked in the same direction.

"You can use those broken bricks as handholds." Colin said. Colin was stupid.

I couldn't, they weren't deep enough to get my fingers into and they were clogged with salt. Instead, I used a metal waste bin to climb onto an adjacent wall and balanced across to the first roof. Mindful not to get my feet caught on rusted razor wire.

Up here, I could see metal supports visible through holes in the roof. I looked at my cousins, then to the ball stuck in a gutter between two sloping units.

I inched forwards. Palms first, rolling my weight across my limbs.

"Come on!" Colin shouted.

I wondered if I could just stop. Crawl out of sight and stay there.

A vibration shuddered through my arm.

What the hell? The tennis ball popped free of the gutter, partly because the gutter was now falling inwards.

The roof tipped away from me. I rolled over, and my feet slammed through the fragile roof. Metal struts snapped, dropping me into the dark interior.

I kept my eyes shut against the pain. Nails pierced my back, three between my ribs and a couple along my spine. Agony flowed through me in cold waves, like the onrush of a harvest tide. I couldn't move, not my hand to reach my phone, or even turn my head to the side.

I heard Sebastian and Colin talking, their voices drifting through the opening in the roof.

"Think he's dead?"

"Hopefully."

"Loser."

"Hey, dick head. If you are still alive, next time your mum runs here, tell her to put some money in your bag."

My belongings rained down through the gaping hole in the roof. Followed by my now empty bag.

At this point, I would have welcomed death.

I lay waiting for something to happen: either enough blood to leak out of my body, or the creeping cold to overwhelm me. Neither of those things happened. I just went numb.

I tried to sit up, but all that happened was that I strained against the nails in my back. God it hurt. There wasn't enough movement to get free. I was stuck.

With nothing else to do, I watched the sky darken. Wondering how long it would take to die, wondering if I could will the onset of blood poisoning.

Above me, the stars twinkled indifferently.

~

The sound of a horse woke me.

Moonlight silvered the sky above and stars shone down casting faint shadows.

My view became blocked by the silhouette of a tall hat, one that would make Dr. Seuss's cat jealous.

"Helloooo!" a voice called. "Anyone down there? Ah, oo. So there is."

A man, as ancient as Methuselah, dropped next to me,

landing lightly. His red riding coat billowed from the fall, and he clutched a walking cane in one hand, to steady his balance.

"You poor fellow. You're pinned to a board dear boy, not quite the notice or poster I would expect. My, my, what is it that Maximillian can do?"

"My phone," I managed, my lips stiff and uncompliant. "Can you call for help? It's in my pocket."

"Yes! Max can help. Certainly!"

He reached in with the expertise of a pickpocket, and brought forth my Nokia.

"Ah. Alas, it appears to be broken."

He turned the handset in his hand, showing me the dead display.

The man sniffed loudly. "Well, maybe I could just give you a hand?"

"Don't," I protested.

His cheeks hollowed as he readied himself to take the strain. With a hand, emaciated and withered, more similar to one of the desiccated mummies I'd seen in the natural history museum, he held mine. Still, there was strength in his grasp. With a sharp jerk, he pulled me from the nails like a cork popping from a champagne bottle.

Once upright, he brushed me down with his spidery fingers. His hand fleetingly caught where a nail had torn into my neck, and came away bloodied.

Distastefully, he rubbed his fingers together.

"It is but a mere scratch."

I tried to reach around to feel the holes in my back, but he shook his head and slapped my hand away.

"How bad is it?"

"You're fine," he said, "It looks worse than it is – you'll have to get a dab of ointment on them, and for now, it's best that you didn't touch them."

I looked at the blank screen on my phone, no cracks in the glass, but no picture either.

The man shrugged out of his coat and wrapped it around my shoulders. I felt warmth start to return to my limbs. My injuries started to tingle.

I tried to take it off, not wanting to get it bloody.

"No, keep it on. It will keep the chill at bay, protect you."

"I just need to get..." what did I need? Had anyone noticed I was gone? Did Mum know, or even care?

"What do you need, dear boy?"

"I don't know."

He looked at my face, at the discoloured bruises left by my dad and the fresh bump from the window pane. He sighed, "Ah, the untold stories of the forgotten. All is not right in your world is it my boy?"

I said nothing.

"You need to meet a friend of mine. A good friend. An artist. He can help."

"What do you mean help?"

"Trust me. Come, we can meet him. Put some ointment on those scratches and clean away some of the scars." He peered out from under the brim of his hat, "What's the matter, you afraid?"

I picked up my bag, surprised that I could actually bend.

"I need to be going." I said.

"But where? What is so pressing that it couldn't wait for another hour? Have you been missed so much that they are out looking for you?"

I shook my head.

"What's your name?"

"Steven."

"I like that. A strong, solid name.

"Steven, I believe that I know someone who can help you, help you with this." He rubbed the flaking blood from his fingers. "What do you say?"

Where else had I to go? No one had come looking. Mum was too much in her own misery to notice I wasn't there. Maybe she thought I'd run away.

Maybe I should.

"Okay."

Max clapped his hands together, "Marvellous."

"I am taking you to The Theatre!" He removed a card from his top pocket and flicked it.

I tried to see, but he turned the card away from me. "My personal invitation. Do not be disturbed by the title, this is no Grand Guignol. The pleasures are far softer. Ahh," he said in reverie, as though savouring a fine wine. "While this is not a place for a fine young man as yourself, it is where the artist is." For an instant, his eyes shone like the setting sun through clouds.

~

Max was quite the eccentric, leading me down different streets looking for the theatre entrance.

I clutched my bag tighter, listening to the sound of the wind blow through broken windows and the overhead telephone cables rattling against their wooden masts.

"I'm sure it was around here somewhere," he said as he dipped to one side and produced a watch from his waistcoat. Max removed his hat and scratched thoughtfully. His silver hair was illuminated gold by the overhead streetlight, like the glass on the dial.

Snapping the watch shut, he set off again, cane rattling against the tarmac every third step.

At last, he stopped before a recessed door. One I'm sure we passed several times, before knocking loudly.

"It's here," he announced.

A hatch slid open, spilling light and sound out into an otherwise empty street. Max produced the invitation and handed it through.

Silently the door opened and a suited doorman beckoned us both inside. Max smiled, tipping his hat.

A wave of warm air hit me, scents of cinnamon, tobacco, the tang of alcohol and something else. My skin prickled with energy.

"Your box is ready, with the usual arrangements, sir," the doorman bowed.

"I will be along in a moment. While I'm sure he would want to see, the show is not for his young eyes." Max leant against his cane, "I take it that Jacque is in his studio?"

"Indeed sir."

"If you would be so good as to tell Isobella to warm my glass, I will be there before the cognac hits the crystal." Max led me down a long corridor with multiple doors leading off. The closest was open and looked to be where the doorman had come from.

Max grinned. "This is the Theatre de la Nuit."

Gas lamps cast flickering pale light across dark oak panels. Off to each side were rooms, each with plaques on their doors. One or two had yellow stars above them.

"Backstage," Max explained, as we walked along. "There are three stages in total, but only ever one in use at any given time."

A door burst open behind me. I turned. Four women, wearing very little but feathered silk, raced into the corridor. Their skin, so pure and unmarred, contrasted against the black of their costumes. I stared. I'd never seen anyone as beautiful, not outside of a magazine. And the way they moved! Sensuous curves carried atop lithe long legs, all hip and sway. The lead girl stopped, and the other three continued into the back of her. I swallowed, watching the Newton's cradle of breast and thigh. Not one of them had a bruise on them.

They laughed, seeing me, mouth agape, before vanishing through a doorway.

I watched after them for a couple of seconds, hoping that they would return.

"No point in loitering in the wings – Madame wouldn't like you spying on her girls. She can be very protective."

Max opened a door and headed up the stairs two at a time. "Jacque works from a different palette."

On the first floor, the windows overlooked a deserted street, misshapen buildings framed by the orange glow of distant streetlights.

Midway down the corridor, brilliant light shone from beneath a closed door. It looked like sunlight, not quite white, but warm and far brighter than the burning lamps that lined the walls.

Max rapped twice on the door.

The light from beneath vanished.

A voice called out, *"Oui? Qu'est-ce?"*

"It's me, Max."

"Bon."

The light returned, then seconds later the door swung open.

Sunlight streamed through an open window that by all rights should have looked deeper into the building, or out onto a dark courtyard below.

Instead rolling green hills undulated away beneath a brilliant azure sky. Birds swooped and soared in the distance above the silhouette of trees on the horizon.

The man standing before it was unassuming, average, save for his beagle eyes and a brown beret. The whiskers down one side of his face were rainbow hued, colours that matched the tips of the digits of his hands.

The man raced to the window, and flipped it over. As it turned, sunlight arced across the room, illuminating a vast array of easels and canvases throughout the room. The new view was that of a night cityscape, resplendent with distant lights sparkling.

"Jacque, I have to leave young Steven in your charge. He could very much do with seeing some of your marvellous paintings." Max dropped a hand onto my shoulder, "Something to bring cheer to his soul, chase his rainclouds away."

Max addressed me quietly, "I will be back within the

hour. You will be safe here." Then he bowed deeply, "Farewell Jacque, until later Steven! The night calls!"

Then he was gone.

At first I thought that the room was tiny. What I'd taken for a wall was a huge Victorian street scene, resplendent with wrought iron lampposts, claustrophobic buildings either side of a cobbled road. Before that there were four smaller canvases stood apart from the others, the largest covered by a sheet.

"Well, Master Steven, I am Jacque LeMarnier," he pushed his fingers through the start of a beard, smearing more pigments into the whiskers.

"Pleased to meet you, sir."

I shrugged out of Max's coat and gingerly felt where the nails had pierced my back, expecting it to be tender. It wasn't. Other than the hole in my clothes, I couldn't actually tell where the nails had gone in. He saw me twisting, shirt tenting wide at a tear, and I glanced down to see my own exposed chest, a mottled patchwork of bruises.

"And these were from tonight?" he pointed to an old one. Or rather, an area my dad labelled his fist magnet.

"It's nothing."

He took a deep breath, then let it out, taking the beret and wiping his forehead.

"Well," he smiled, "let me show you something." Standing he gestured to the scattered pictures around the room.

He motioned to the painting of a woman. I'd heard people use the expression that it was so realistic the eyes followed you. This was on the next level. I was looking at the bare back and shoulders of a woman, raven hair spilling down the side of her face. As I stepped closer to get a better look, she turned away from me, the strap of her dress falling from her shoulder.

"How did you do that?" No cables ran into the frame, I couldn't see power lights, it had to be video.

"This is Anna, my wife. At least how I remember her, she watches over me while I paint." He picked up a dark green drape and gently hung it over the frame. The woman in the picture turned and blew him a kiss before she disappeared from view. He touched his fingers to his lips, and pressed them against the folds of the sheet.

"How...?"

"Do you believe in magic?" he smiled. "Sometimes if you wish for something, if you wish for it with all your heart, you can capture it. Draw down your soul and work with it. With me, it's painting." He gestured around the room, "These are my wishes."

We walked around the room and Jacque pointed to the night scene that I'd taken for a window, "Paris by night. The one on the back is my father's farm in Montpelier. Good memories."

I must have pulled a face as his next question was, "Do you have good memories of home?"

I didn't like where this was going. "Some."

He nodded.

"What's that one over there?" I pointed to the largest covered painting.

"That will be a portrait of Madame Morte, the owner of this place."

"Can I have a look?"

"*Non*. It's not started yet."

Jacque picked up a pallet knife and mixing plate. "I have to work on this street scene. You can help me." He worked quickly, sometimes turning the picture at the window to check the colours in daylight.

I mixed paints and cleaned brushes. I wondered if anyone had missed me yet. If Sebastian and Colin had told them what had happened.

While I worked, Jacque fixed a new canvas into a metal frame.

"Paint it with this, both sides. Do not touch surface." He passed me a bucket of black, pure darkness.

It looked evil.

"Is it poisonous?"

The tips of my fingers prickled, as they got closer to the surface.

"*Non, il va manger vos doigts!*"

"Sorry, what did you say?"

"Don't touch! It will... leave finger marks." I didn't think that was quite what he said.

I worked at his side, marvelling at the layers he built up. Outlines became defined, patches refined to recognisable shapes, only to be covered over by another layer. I watched him go over the same area with different solid hues, only for it to be smudged with a hand or fingers. Occasionally he would flick wine on the oils from his cup, or stop to take a long draught.

I felt my eyes close, arms aching from mixing pot after pot.

He smiled. "Rest in the corner if you want? I've nearly finished this, and then I can start yours."

Jacque reached into the painting, turning a valve on the nearest lamppost. The flames in the picture died to glowing embers, casting shadows about the room.

Eyes just about closed now, I could see him start to work.

"What are you doing?" I asked, fighting sleep.

"Painting a picture for you."

I looked at the thick layer of blue that he had added in the centre.

"What is it?"

"This is a place where I used to go, my escape. It's a piece of sky."

~

Only half opening my eyes, I saw that a rejuvenated Max had returned. Where before he had been white haired and emaciated, now his face was free from wrinkles and a thick, black, mane curled from beneath his hat.

"Ah, there he is. Time to get you back where you can be found."

Jacque took the canvas, folded it and carefully placed it into a frame.

"Here," Jacque said, "is a means to escape whatever you want. Close your eyes, believe. *Croire.*" I heard the zip go on my bag. "Keep it safe."

I tried to stand, but couldn't.

"Sleep." Max instructed.

I don't remember exactly how I got back to the industrial unit, only fragments. I remember looking up at Max, or at least at this new version, and later Max brushing his hand along the rafter as though smoothing a blanket. I heard nails bouncing off walls.

He lay me down, back where I fell.

My phone beeped, there was a gentle tap of onscreen keys and the haptic buzz, then nothing.

Blackness.

~

When I opened my eyes, I thought I was looking up into one of Jacque's paintings: the picture of sky that he'd painted me. But he wouldn't have framed it with rusted iron or asbestos. And there wouldn't be two ugly familiar faces leering down at me.

They jerked out of the way.

I sat up and a rag fell off my chest, threadbare and decayed. Stray fibres clung to the rafter beneath me and where I lay was stained by blood or rust.

Dad burst through a door, falling over debris in the process, and Mum followed after, crying, sweeping me into her arms Everything was all right. If only it could have stayed like that. To be held; to be loved was all I ever wanted.

~

Over a period of a month, the arguments started again. The shock of nearly losing me had only united them temporarily.

I closed my eyes and sat beneath the painting, shutting out the noise of their fighting. In my head, I sought imagined bird song, wanting, wishing it to get louder.

"You can't leave me. You leave me and you're dead!" I heard him shout. "If I walk, I go out of that door and I'm not coming back!"

A slight breeze touched my face, followed by the scent of maple and blossom.

Solid footfalls sounded on the stairs, not dampened by the carpet.

The door to my bedroom crashed open. I jumped. Even though I expected him to come into my room, the ferocity frightened me.

He glared. His knuckles were cracked and swollen. I dropped my gaze, not wanting to meet his, in case he took that to be a sign of defiance.

His ragged breathing slowed, and I could hear him swallow, a dry, feverish click. Risking a glance, I saw that he was watching me.

Dad flipped a book from my shelf into the floor. I'd arranged them in order of importance.

Compensation gifts from Mum.

Works of James Herbert and Shaun Hutson hit the floor. A spider that had been hiding behind one managed to survive the drop and scuttled backwards to the base of the bookcase.

A rare Clive Barker followed, one of five hundred.

He was goading me, wanting me to react. Blood thudded through my ears and I could feel heat radiating from my face.

"Look-ie here. Isn't this one of your favourites?" A pristine *Christine*. I'd only read that one once, carefully bending the cover outwards to minimize the stress on the binding.

He folded it over in two, and then tore it apart. Both halves dropped onto the increasing pile.

His smile faded. He was no longer looking for a reaction for me, more intent on wholesale destruction of my prized possessions.

I looked at the painting, seeing the open blueness of the sky, wishing myself there, under the tranquillity, away from this, away from everything.

All I could hear was the sound of tearing paper, and somewhere in the background, Mum sobbing.

She wasn't dead. Hurt.

She'd given up. Given up on herself and given up on me.

"You little shit! Why don't you cry!?" he snarled.

I wondered what I'd done wrong. What I could have done to make him so angry?

There would be no reasoning, he wanted me to suffer, and that was all.

The spider had made a tentative run, taking advantage of the break. It scuttled away from the bookcase, but bumped into Dad's shoe. It was a regular house spider, brown with tan stripes. I could see its black eyes reflecting light from the picture.

The picture - it was getting brighter.

My dad turned, I caught a whiff of his beery breath and the pungent tang of stale sweat, and his eyes fixed on the source of the light – seeing it for the first time.

He took a step forward. The spider, suddenly exposed, ran towards the centre of the room, towards me.

Dad took the picture in his hands, turning it over, as confused as I had been.

I moved, launching myself at him, meaning to wrest it from his grasp.

I didn't even feel the blow that threw me against the shelves. The unit cracked back against the wall and I felt two ribs break, before I fell onto the slew of papers.

Triumphantly, he held the painting above his head.

He drank in my sorrow. I was crying. Everything good in the world was gone.

He slammed the frame into the floor and it shattered. The canvas buckled and warped, slightly unfolding.

I could see the spider alter its direction, as it turned towards the fresh reservoir of darkness ahead.

Although clouded by tears, I saw. I saw the spider run into the blackness, its speck of a body spiralling away into a void.

I clutched my side. Hoping that Dad hadn't seen it, making as much noise as I could, anything to distract him from looking at the canvas.

I cried a world away.

~

It didn't take long for him to fall asleep, another couple of cans of beer in front of the television. I carefully picked up the painting, holding it by the bare material. On one side, the blue sky continued to shine, blowing air at my feet, the other was an inky mirror of blackness, sucking towards my legs as I carried it downstairs.

Fury made me silent.

I walked around the side of the chair, next to the table where he had emptied the contents of his pockets.

His eyes flicked open, and he looked at me. There was

a complete lack of comprehension there, he saw me and smiled. I wonder if he saw his hate reflected, stored in a reservoir and now breaking through the dam.

I threw the black canvas over him. It wrapped around his head, sinking to his shoulders.

He stood. His heels kicked the chair and his hands waved through the space his head should have occupied.

A beheaded chicken, he thrashed, falling and slamming and crashing against the floor. Where the blackness touched the chair, it became worn and abraded.

I dropped behind the settee, listening to the banging and crashes getting louder. A lamp fell over. The television exploded, showering glass and sparks into the room.

Then it fell silent.

"Steven!" I heard Mum shout. "Steven!"

I looked over the edge to see the rest of my dad being pulling into the dark, toes drumming against the floorboards, until they too were gone.

Holding my side, I picked up his keys and wallet and dropped them in.

I carefully folded the canvas and slid it under the chair. I'd hide it in my bedroom later.

I hurried to the front door and threw it wide.

Mum came into the living room, standing like a spectre at the threshold, looking as though she didn't believe he was gone. Looking at me, then at the open doorway.

She didn't ask what happened, and I didn't tell her.

She stood on the front step looking out into the night. I put my hand in hers and she said nothing.

The wind buffeted the door wanting to close it on my lie, but there was something out there... Barely audible above the night's murmur I could make out an indistinct tap-tapping. Mum heard it too. Her fingers tightened around mine.

A wave of relief washed over me as a familiar man in a red coat rounded the corner, walking along the street towards our house. As he reached the end of our path he smiled at us. "*Bonsoir*" he said whilst tapping the brim of his hat with his cane. Mum muttered an embarrassed greeting before walking inside. Max winked at me and I smiled back at him before he carried on, whistling to himself. I watched him round the corner and then was gone.

I continued to smile as I closed the door.

She's in my bowels, weaving her magic, cutting... creating. And when her people thunder the boards, I am lightning beneath their britches, a storm within their boots. I gild the performers' vibrant lilies, causing Madame to shiver. The audience does not bear witness to my Lady's shudder but they sense the frisson with every flicker of lust-scented candle. For she, and I – we entice. For our own amusement.

Just don't tell; never tell.

Byron Longshanks guards my doors. He came here to *steal pretty things* back in the day. The dancers and I watched from within as he played with my locks, fiddling and jiggling them with ebony fingers. I giggled at his tickle. He thought himself clever. Strong and streetwise he most certainly was but intelligence had, and still has, no home in the head of our beautiful Byron. Seven feet tall, dressed in rags – regularly collected and incarcerated for minor crimes, for surviving – he needed saving. So we sent him a rumour. And now he's ours.

People wander back and forth. Some stop, frown; they hear the music without hearing, sense the dance... then leave. A morsel of longing, of regret will render them weak for days hereafter. Others – the ones we've been waiting for – linger, translucent invitations burning against their legs or slowly caressing their cleavage. They wish to cross my threshold but I offer no obvious entrance. Our visitors don't even know how they reached this faded part of London except they've been dreaming of my opulence, of who they might meet within my private walls, the famous and infamous – unaware it is our reputation that has drawn them here, licking at their minds as they slept, teasing raw nerves with burlesque promises. They *have* arrived, and that's what's important. There is no need to remember the route. Next time, if they get a next time, they will find themselves back here, dressed and ready, the journey irrelevant.

We watch them now as they fathom out their confusion, observe how they ignore the lost and the lonely who stagger past on their way to this squat for that fix, oblivious to our lush magnificence; unseeing.

Too cruel, we have dallied with our guests overly long. They *are* invited, after all. We must show them the door, allow them to experience *the shift*. Byron waits as the transformation, the slow realisation happens. He has learned the art of patience. Once in, he will steal their pretty hearts.

Most of our neighbours are boarded-up with no souls

of their own. We do not allow them to leech off ours – it would be the beginning of the end, though they've tried. Fingers of mould seeping into my flesh, hurting my foundations with arthritic damp they pushed and they crumbled and let me believe I was done for, but what am I if not the Theatre de la Nuit, and capable of defending myself against more magic than a mere brick erection can throw at me.

To my left, the construction wears its skeleton on the outside; metal poles that sing discordant melodies. To my right, a once-grand restaurant bears its tattoos in shame; its windows broken behind unforgiving metal shutters. We are connected by party walls alone, but only we are giving a party.

And so we survive – like Byron, our skin intact, our countenance most exquisitely divine.

Our audience may smoke, if they wish. And many do. Fat cigars are a favourite, the like of which have been rolled upon Cuban thighs. The sweet stench is part of the fabric, never stale. The room sparkles too with the glimmer and glamour of long cigarette holders. Thin black cheroots or exotic blends rolled into coloured papers protruding from silver-plated ends. How we love this pretension.

We have regulars; one wonders if some ever leave, as though they have forgotten how or believe they have signed a contract of perpetual attendance, a commitment to spend, spend, spend misbegotten lucre as easily as they spill their sorrows. These permanent fixtures wander the floor, unfixed. Forever in a state of surprise, they behave as though every encounter, every performance or transaction is their very first. It is a strange condition. As long as their presence amongst the silk-suited dandies who sashay alongside heavy-booted *garçonnes* does not disturb, as long as their somewhat tired and dishevelled appearance does not startle the starlets that hang off swaggering barrow boys' arms, then we are content. We allow it.

Some pay to get onto the Guest List. There is a different price for each and every one of them, never to be revealed. Instead there is talk of privilege. There is talk of class and of entitlement, none of which holds sway. And when the lie is told that the list is full, it always amuses us how swiftly the begging begins. The more they beg, the more it costs. If only they knew that for every paying guest, another – one of considered choosing – can enter for free. But no-one ever asks. Inequality is left at the door.

Red is the carpet upon which guests tread and red is the velvet that supports derrières and red is the stage curtain which hangs in trembling readiness. I pulse with it. And on nights when passions rise at the same rate as the flurrying petticoats I feel those shades of red course and stream within me, ready to burst up and rain down, to drench our semi-copulating invitees. Such is the blissful pain. I keep it, however, in check. One should never drown one's guests; it is so bad for business.

Opening time approaches, though time itself, as a concept, as a method of order, is somewhat transient here. L'ouverture happens when it happens. It is not dictated by the chime of a clock. The only concession is the dull clang of our gong which announces the start of proceedings, the first performance. It is used at the end of the interval to hush the talk as on stage corsets are tightened, décolletages exposed, and the performers are ready to share their art once again. Only when whispers and breathy promises are silenced can the tap and the stamping feet resume their work, can singers pour out their liquid song. Meerla, our mute Russian timpanist is responsible for the gong. Without him, nothing can start. He pounds it now; just the once. Politicians still their fingers on young partners' waists; bishops and lovers release each other from tongue-twisting embraces. A mixed brew of the beautiful and the dangerous take their seats, expectations distilled into a toxic sea of desire. My innards vibrate with the tension, the excitement; audience to one side, artists hidden away from sight on the other. They are the spleen to my liver and vice-versa.

Someone coughs; another utters a boudoir-bound gasp.

The Theatre de la Nuit falls quiet.

Let us end the trepidation.

Let us declare the curtain... open.

TERRY GRIMWOOD teaches electrical installation at a college, is an amateur dramatic ham and playwright, publisher (theEXAGGERATEDpress and Wordland), harmonica player and blues singer, writer of text books and teller of tall tales. His novels are *Axe* (Double Dragon), *Bloody War* (Eibonvale) and *The Places Between* (Pendragon). He also has two collections of short stories out there, called *The Exaggerated Man* (thEXAGGERATEDpress) and *There is a Way to Live Forever* (Black Shuck Books). There are more novellae on the way!

GUY RUSSELL was born in Chatham and lives in Milton Keynes. Work in *Brace* (Comma), *Troubles Swapped For Something Fresh* (Salt), *Between Worlds*, Liar's League, and elsewhere. Comp wins: HE Bates Award; Northern Stories; Leicester Poetry; Flash500; Redwing; Cannon.

V. F. LESANN is a co-writing team presently living in Alberta, Canada, comprised of Leslie Van Zwol and Megan Fennell. Court clerks by day and writers of strange tales by night, they have both dabbled in various styles of dance but won't confirm rumours of being back-up dancers at the Theatre de la Nuit. They have previously been published in *Sirens* and *Equus* (World Weaver Press), as well as individually in various publications, including EDGE Publishing's *Tesseracts* anthologies.

DAVID TURNBULL is Scottish by birth but has lived in

London most of his adult life. He is a member of the Clockhouse London group of genre writers. He write mainly short fiction and has had numerous short stories published in magazines and anthologies. He can be found at **www.tumsh.co.uk**

ROSIE SEYMOUR has had a number of short stories published online and has written for *Mslexia* magazine . She has a short story in the *Terror Tales of the Scottish Highlands* collection. Rosie lives in the Lake District with the author Simon Kurt Unsworth and their collection of children and animals. In real life Rosie is a nurse.

GARY BUDGEN grew up and still lives in London, UK. He has been published in magazines such as *Interzone, Dark Horizons, Morpheus Tales,* and *Theaker's Quarterly* as well as many anthologies. Recent stories can be found in *We Can Improve You* from Boo Books, *Pyromania* from Thirteen O'Clock Press and *Sensorama* from Eibonvale Press. He is a member of London Clockhouse Writers. His website is **www.garybudgen.wordpress.com**

HAYLEY ORGILL lives in Derby with her writing fiancé of 17 years (well, you've got to be sure!). Hayley has only really started to submit short stories in the last few years, but has been writing privately for some time. She runs the monthly Derby Quad Writing Circle and enjoys meeting up with likeminded people, so you will often find her at local writing conventions. 'The Show Must Go

On' is her third published short story and is waiting for three more short stories to be published as well as currently working several other big projects.

When spare time occasionally raises its head, Hayley enjoys reading, and loves nothing more than stories with a twist... probably due to an unhealthy love of *Tales of the Unexpected* and the set of *Pan Book of Horrors* she collected at an obscenely early age.

JOHN WINTER is a complex individual, whose perfect wife describes him as high maintenance, He has been sighted wandering through woods, talking to wooden eagles for inspiration and taking photos of the remote English countryside.

LILY CHILDS has an obsession with misunderstood demons and takes unsavoury delight in Victorian underworlds, twisted myths and the necrotic. 'Underbelly', her contribution to the mysterious story of *Madame Morte* is told by the Theatre de la Nuit itself, where the dark, debauched and dissolute tread its boards – by invitation only.

Lily's dark horror, crime and ghost stories have been published by KnightWatch Press, Crystal Lake Publishing, The Sinister Horror Company, Ganglion Press, Western Legends Publishing and James Ward Kirk Fiction. She has recently completed a supernatural asylum novel. A second gallows novel hangs in the balance.

This is PIXIE's first dip in the pool that is editing and it to say it has been a 'journey' is the biggest understatement of all understatements in the whole of understatement land. When she began this project she was a jobbing Theatre Artist whose biggest daily highlight was following the staff of the supermarkets around to see what would land in the reduced section. Since then she has become a teacher of Acting and Performing Arts at Bilborough 6th Form College, has directed shows as part of the National Theatre Connections project and has learned to repeat herself several times, often within the same breath, information she has no idea how she retains.

She continues her professional practice as an actor, facilitating sessions for the University of Nottingham's Medical School and designing and delivering bespoke workshops. She has links with Derby Theatre and Nottingham Playhouse as well as many independently funded theatre companies around the region.

In her 'spare' time she is a member of the board of trustees for Derbyshire LGBT+ and part of the fundraising team for Derbyshire Pride.

She lives with her ever patient partner, son and hyperactive Yorkshire Terrier aptly named 'Scruff'. She is partial to stealing her granddaughter, when her daughter isn't looking and wrangling furniture in the name of 'Interior Design'.

She is perhaps best known, however, for her ability to obtain money (with and (sometimes) without menaces) in exchange for brightly coloured pieces of paper with bold numbers printed on them.